# PARTISANS

# PARTISANS

## a lost work by

# Geoffrey
# Peerson Leed

*M. Allen Cunningham*

M. ALLEN CUNNINGHAM

ATELIER26 : SAMIZDAT SERIES
Northwest Territory

Cover design and additional artistry by Nathan Shields
Book design by M.A.C.

isbn-13: 978-0-9893023-4-0
isbn-10: 0989302342

Library of Congress Control Number: 2015901352

A26 *samizdat series* Vol.3

With thanks to the Corporation of Yaddo.

Atelier26 Books are printed in the U.S.A. on acid-free paper.

Atelier26

*"A magnificent enthusiasm, which feels
as if it never could do enough to reach
the fullness of its ideal; an unselfishness
of sacrifice, which would rather cast
fruitless labour before the altar than
stand idle in the market."* —John Ruskin

Atelier26Books.com

for
those
who
work
in the
dark

# PARTISANS

It is the difficulty that unites us — the difficulty of making the intangible tangible, of creating a cold form to contain our fervent content. All of us know that difficulty so profoundly that we would all recognize its nature despite the totally different considerations that fill our pauses.
—JOHN BERGER, *A Painter of Our Time*


Some few wandering Hasids go into exile in order 'to suffer exile with the Shekinah,' the presence of God in the world — which is, as you have doubtless noticed, lost or strayed. The man who is detached in this way is the friend of God, 'as the stranger is the friend of another stranger on account of their strangeness on earth.'
—ANNIE DILLARD


Hate-hardened heart, O heart of iron,
iron is iron till it is rust.
There never was a war that was
not inward; I must
fight till I have conquered in myself what
causes war, but I would not believe it.
I inwardly did nothing.
O Iscariot-like crime!
Beauty is everlasting
And dust is for a time.
—MARIANNE MOORE, "In Distrust of Merits"

Let us stand here and admit that we have no road.
Being everything, let us admit that is to be something.
Or give ourselves the benefit of the doubt.
—WILLIAM EMPSON


I can't recall an end at all, any end I ever, can't,
any, demise, no —
cause maybe —
maybe I … never ended?
—ALI SMITH, *How to be both*

# EDITOR'S NOTE

The manuscript of this lost work by Geoffrey Peerson
Leed came to me through strange and circuitous means,
a story too involved — and involving too many actors
— to recount here. Moreover, I am unable to properly
thank those most instrumental in making this
publication possible: to name them would surely put
them at risk. Suffice it to say that Leed, whom I never
met personally, remains a ghostly neighbor of kinds: I
work, as he did, here in the Northwest Territory.

   The Leed archives now in my possession are
extensive, with *Partisans* accounting for a great portion
of that material (there is also a body of correspondence
recuperated from Bureau files). Unfortunately, even in
their entirety the archives can shed no real light on the
circumstances of Leed's disappearance. While I and my
compatriots have our suspicions, the truth is that Leed's
fate, like much of his life, was and must remain a
mystery.

   Of primary importance is Leed's resolve in the face
of all that opposed him and his work. *Partisans*, being a
foundational document of the Literary Resistance,
constitutes a record of that resolve. When I think of

Leed's defiance against the times in which he struggled, I remember these words by Havel: "[A] post-totalitarian system [is] built on foundations laid by the historical encounter between dictatorship and the consumer society. ... [But] every free expression of life indirectly threatens the post-totalitarian system politically."

This samizdat edition of *Partisans* is presented in its nine dialectical parts according to Leed's designs, as indicated in manuscripts discovered after his disappearance. Titles are Leed's own. The text has not been altered, except for minor annotations and addenda, which I include in the hope that readers may assist with recovering some of the references that have been lost.

—M.A.C., *Northwest Territory*

# THE
# MANUSCRIPT

# 1.

# In Country

There were three of us this morning,
I'm the only one this evening,
But I must go on.

—"The Partisan," folk song

They came pushing across the border on several fronts. They had vowed to do this, had warned of it, and now they were everywhere in the villages. Hiding in a basement he watched their tromping boots, dark in the opaque windowglass above. At night all was a slurry of sound. Patrolling, patrolling.

There was a scuffle the second morning. Gunfire. Footsteps in flight — a woman's feet, he thought. Screams. Tanks boomed south of the square and he heard the muffled crackle of buildings crumbling.

He remained burrowed under the basement stairs.

He would wait and try to sense the growing fires outside, the smoke that would curl along the street, a hand cupped over him, so he could hold his breath and run, the empty pistol in his trousers waist.

He would head for the rendezvous point, vanish again. If he was not mowed down amid the buildings he would run for the wood beyond the graveyard, the dugout where in summer he'd drunk wine in earthen cups, clashing his to the rims of others and laughing, alive and furious with the joy of brotherhood, the beautiful freedom of work and rest, food and sleep. Non-allegiance. Those were the days before X betrayed them, before they all turned their lives over to an oath and made themselves betrayable.

Now he could scent the smoke.

His fingers found the cold metal at his waist.

Running in the street moments later, head down and willing himself invisible, he felt X beside him keeping pace. Old friend. They could be anyone, each of them, running for any reason or cause. He felt Dobo beside him also, and Finn — double-crossed or not, martyrs or not, it didn't matter now, even they were again themselves, before the war made them symbols. They were, all of them, free of betrayal, the cause, the creeds. Comrade, traitor, retribution: words couldn't warp them anymore. They were running along together, Jude felt, shoulder to shoulder under the smoke, out of step, a ragged music of feet.

Actually, of course, he was alone.

In the room with X before the bloodspray, they had talked very quietly. The red of the old woman's brains stained the hearthstone. A broken light moved in the glassless windows, made seafoam of the broken glass on the floor. The trees outside were tossing.

Jude stood for a time in the doorway, his back against the post, one foot at either side of the threshold. But X was sitting and Jude was finally drawn to the equilibrium of a chair. The cane seat creaked, putting the moment in order. The old woman's ceramic servingware lay wrecked about their feet. Clumps of her white hair were scattered over the floor.

They were sitting so close their knees almost touched. X slumped back with hands slack on his thighs, at ease, or anyway resigned. His clear dark eyes met Jude's in a peaceable look — contentment almost, or a kind of blank satisfaction at having matters at last decided. The sealed moment before them allowed them to be merely men again. Lifelong neighbors.

What did they talk about? Jude tried to remember.

The trees had hissed and stooped. He had heard the wind whistling upstairs.

It wasn't that they made peace, or came to an understanding, or begged and gave forgiveness. Whatever kind of men they were, they were dealt requirements. They were flesh but also action.

So when the time came Jude leaned and X closed his eyes as the barrel touched his brow.

The shot seemed to smash the ceramic all over again, to shatter anew the windswept windows. X's head whipped back, then dropped. He listed in his seat and his shoulders seemed to crumple inward. On the gray stone behind him young blood and brains splashed over the old woman's.

Jude, till then, had forgotten how young they all still were.

The old woman was to be their liaison across the border. Dobo had found her by his reliable means. For about a month they'd been staging incursions, eating away at the northernmost line of the offensive, at pains to appear tenfold their actual number. What they saw while setting charges on rail grades or penetrating encampments, disguised, to lay mines was a force that swelled each day by thousands. From a ridgetop one night Jude watched a great river of camplights stretching away to the south. Against such enormity, what were he and his comrades fighting for? And what was it that animated the awful Army below? Thoughts, he decided. Something in the mind. An idea of order, destiny, happiness.

In her stone cottage by the border the little old woman hid Dobo and the other three. Her husband had died some years ago, before the war. They had married and set up house long before the present border was drawn. Their people, she explained, were never of this side or that side. They were of the hills, that's all. There they lived and roamed, drew water of the streams, farmed the valleys, shepherded along the slopes and highlands. You cannot make a straight line over these mountains, she said, and swatted the air. No, absurd.

She took in washing ever since her husband's passing. She washed for some of the officers encamped in the village beyond her woods. Dobo and the men would be safe in her garret, she said, very safe, right over the Army's head. Dobo agreed. They made beds of their coats and lay down beneath her cobwebbed rafters. Each slept by his gun.

The second night, X went out on reconnaissance. It was daybreak before he came back, his left hand mangled in blood, to tell how they'd nearly caught him in the woods. A bullet had torn his thumb off. He'd dug himself under and prayed. Jude and the others had guessed him dead but he'd only lost a thumb. They tousled his leaf-matted hair, kissed him, congratulated. The washerwoman brought them alcohol and they cleaned the hand, stitched it and dressed it. She swabbed his blood from the wooden stairs.

I accomplished nothing, X said.

They told him to rest. Dobo would go out tonight.

But within the hour they were hearing voices below, then boots clomping up the narrow stairwell, and the four in the garret were plunging toward the soffit opening, kicking out the screen, worming through legs-first to drop from the eave into the old woman's beet patch. Jude was first to land. He turned amazed to find no soldiers awaiting, a clear way to the woods. But some were coming around the house so he fired to hold them off. There were eight or more. Their automatic rifles blazed. Nothing for it but to run.

Finn had landed, and here came Dobo dropping with a thump. They both staggered up with olive tunics smeared in blood and he thought them done for but remembered the beets. He was well within the trees already and turned again just as the rifles laid them open. Blood burst in blurred silhouette against the side of the house. Their bodies melted in the garden leaves.

X dropped from the soffit into the heap of flesh.

Not that one! called a voice, and the guns ceased.

Jude was well ahead of any pursuit. He would run till strength failed him.


This was one thing X talked about later, before the bloodspray, after they'd come back to that broken cottage — Jude remembered now:

The Colonel has my thumb. I watched him wrap it in a kerchief and put the little bundle in a shirt pocket. Not that he'd done much to earn it, hadn't even shot it off himself. No, that was my duty, used my own gun. He stood and watched. A test like. Once I did it I was on the floor howling like a dog. He patted his pocket and told me to remember. He still wouldn't trust me. He meant he owned me now. Live or die, his decision. They weren't going to follow me right back, they were going to come in the morning. But he didn't trust me. I feared him too much and he knew it. When I first went to him — to tell him what I'd do — it was fear that led me there. And the same fear has betrayed me now. You should be more afraid, you know. What will you do after this?

I don't know.

He'll take a hatchet to your cock, that man.

No, I'm not afraid.

Hm. Funny, you know, but neither am I. Right now, here with you. I know what you will do, my brother, and I'm not afraid.

Good, you shouldn't be. We are old friends, whatever has happened.

I believe you. I know you mean it.

Yes. Let's sit here awhile longer.

# OLD WOMAN

*They push through the door. Suddenly they are everywhere in my house. Breaking things, stomping about.*

*You have them upstairs, they tell me. I do not deny this. I say nothing. It is ending now, I feel it. They do not bother to point their guns. They want to be powerful, fearsome, guns or no.*

*They take me by the wrists. They are stomping upstairs some of them. I do not fight these ones below, I say nothing. They begin to shove me about, their hands like clamps and my wrists all but broken where the arthritis throbs. They begin to smash cups, plates. They overturn the table my husband made. They are in our house and whatever they can occupy or break is theirs, sign of their strength. They brought the war to the mountains, the village, and now they carry it through my door.*

*No more hiders for you washerwoman. One behind me seizes my hair. I feel the ending now as he yanks and rips and the others smash the pictures, the vase, the mirror.*

*Gunfire upstairs, outside.*

*They are dragging me down and I say nothing. They mean to smash me, to do it without guns. To the hearthstone now I see it coming. I do not so much as whisper.*

. . .

Now Jude was running in the burning village, coughing in the smoke. And now he realized he would not run to the dugout. Surely X had divulged it. There'd be no one to meet, whoever had returned there was dead by now. The few others would scatter. The resistance, he saw, was over. And X was not to blame. X had but sped along the inevitable. You resist or die, and they were dead, or would soon be so.

Coming to the far edge of the square, out of the smoke, Jude passed a moving convoy. It was traveling away from him. He slowed to a walk, kept his eyes on the ground. The engines in the transports whirred on at full pitch. He was not shouted at to stop. But as he crossed into the pastures at the limits of town there were columns of troops ahead, marching toward him. He wouldn't try his luck a second time. He'd noticed a culvert off the road. He veered that way without a thought, knowing he'd draw attention. Then he was stooped over in the shoulder-high tunnel and plashing through water up to his knees, ramming forward into darkness, running again.

The war was charging west. He would go the other way.

. . .

He was long in the forest, crossing east. There were many brooks and little mountain lakes. He drank from these with a cup from the old woman's house. A clayware cup, once a goblet, the stem had broken off and the rim was deeply chipped on one side, but somehow the soldiers had not smashed it altogether. He had found very little else of use left there. A triangular shard of mirror (he would try everyday to look himself in the eyes); a swathe of cotton drapery — for bandage, sunguard, sling, or sack (he wore it sash-wise at his waist, the empty pistol shoved snug); a queer hat with a brim that buttoned to the crown on both sides (it was sweat-stained; the dead husband's?); a torn section of a page from the Bible (the sole scrap of paper in the house); and under the woman's sink basin, gray and mice-nibbled, a heel of stale bread, so wooden he thought it the toe of a sabot at first. The Army had of course raped her garden, but after much digging in the soil where Dobo and Finn had bled he turned up a small handful of pumpkin seeds.

The bread he'd half-eaten — painstakingly sucked on really — while hiding in that basement in the village. His first day out he ate the rest beside a pond, having soaked the crust in his cup — drank it, more like, for it made a spongy soup. The seeds were finished the following night.


He walked through red-floored forest. In the higher places there were little mounds of snow here and there at the feet of trees, pristine white. Sweating, mosquito-ridden, he scooped with his hands, filled his mouth, let the icy melt flow deliciously over his tongue and flood the dark pockets of his cheeks, down his beard. His diseased teeth ached. He topped his cup and stood it before him in the pine needles where he sat. It gleamed crystalline, white. Then, very slowly, a blueness came into it. Greenness. And finally it had darkened to the clay color of the cup itself. The new water, in appearing, never rippled.

In the woods he foraged for berries, sorrel, pine nuts. He wouldn't starve though hunger was constant. He could hardly believe the silence, the birdcalls, clatter of leaves. The war was everywhere but it wasn't here.

In some places the trees cleared to meadow or escarpment and he could see villages below, or towns in the distance. Cathedral spires. Everywhere the crawling of troops over the green-brown land, all silent at this height.

One morning he sat on a rocky outcropping watching black banners of smoke arise from a city far below. Along the tiny highways transports came and went, invading, fleeing. They felt their own speed, they roared at their throttles, but from here the vastness of the picture slowed them, and noise that deafened down there was dissolved in the expanse — silent, gone, of no consequence. Jude, on his crag, could have been a pale star remote beyond the reach of what he saw. He could take the shard of mirror and flash it, a kind of reminder to the war-gripped below. Of course he didn't.

Maybe he was dead already and this remoteness an afterlife — or a dream before it. He'd never expected streets of gold, a robe fringed with light, to find himself winging among fleecy clouds.

To walk, hide, be hungry — that seemed fitting. A form of happiness, perhaps, after all he'd done and seen.

*Josepha, though, he'd never harmed.*

*She collected cigarette cards — portraits of the Chief Commander. She gummed them to the wall beside her bed, in little rows. This was in the earliest months of the war, when the Chief Command still bothered with propaganda, before power shifted completely in its favor.*

*She fed him sweetbreads from the cooling oven trays, apricots from her family's village in the east. She lay beside him, watching him eat. He sprinkled crumbs on her naked belly, a mad confectioner. She laughed and he watched the divots of shadow near her collarbone. He would kiss those places first.*

*Why do you love him? he asked her, glancing at the little bedside gallery.*

*She simpered, sucking at her lips. She was very young. The cause is what I love, she said. The unity. I love knowing that nothing can stop it. The hour is now. The force of history is with us. She'd begun to smirk, a haughtiness beyond her years, her words borrowed from the broadcasts, the posters that lined every street in that precinct. She was everything the*

Chief Command could hope for in the people, and there were tens of thousands like her. By use of that vulnerability the Command could make the cause invincible.

He went with her to one of the earliest marches. Never had he been in such a crowd. Their chants were deafening. Afterward, energized, she tackled him on the pantry floor, threw her shoulders back and rode him like a dancer in a craze. Flour coated the boards beneath them. Their skin as they rolled took on the ghostly pall.

What side are you on? she would ask him in time. But she knew, as he did, that their hours together were a kind of dream, where sides were no matter.

He had believed in her after all. Somehow he believed even still.

Jude's path descended. He began to find blazemarks in the hemlocks and pines, trails scored for carrying water, for leading goats or oxen to higher pasture. But it was still a long way down to the nearest village, a day's walk at least.

At a turning under a bower of ivy and wild wisteria he came upon a ruined shrine. A miniature church of kinds, it was sized to house a reduced icon or saint, a kneeler, a candelabra maybe. There were small windows of stained glass, most of the color caked dark in dirt. Coming to the front Jude was surprised by the sight of a spidery little woman squatting inside in black skirts. She held a lacy sunshade in one hand. Her eyes were blacked in heavy grease, elongated at the corners Egyptian-wise. They jerked up at him.

Shoot or rob me, which is it? she said.

By the voice he understood she was a man. Then he saw the stubble, dark at the jaws and gray about the chin.

No, he said, remembering the pistol at his waist. Gun's empty. Only good as a hammer now.

She pointed to his feet. Don't stand there. Her voice was very deep and creaked at the edges. My baby's under that sod.

He stepped back. He looked but could make out no grave. He asked was the shrine the baby's, but she didn't hear. She was rocking on her heels where she squatted. The sunshade was torn and the bare tines tapped at the windows on each side.

Don't you tell me I killt her. You're no one to say so.

No. How did she die?

By death. It came and got her out of my arms. I was holding her hard, no different than her mama before she died. I held her like mama did but she wouldn't feed. I told her mama couldn't no more. Death won't nurse, soldiers make it so.

She touched her man-chest.

I showed her the tit. I was all sore with milk but she wouldn't take. She shrank every day.

Jude said, You did your best.

I'm a good mother. The Army starved the villagers. Killed them, the ones left. I carried her here for our food. She could only breathe small. I gave her bark to suck, berry juice, she wouldn't swallow. I put leaves in her mouth, I stuffed her mouth full, she was white, her eyes, she wouldn't chew. I fed her more but she wouldn't. Don't tell me I failed her.

No, said Jude. You're a good mother.

She looked up. Her man-eyes were blue and bulging, an agony of color. Aren't you cold? she said. Aren't you soaked to the ribs?

Jude glanced above into the canopy of sunshot pine. Insects glimmered and swirled.

She said, The ponds'll flood, the rains won't stop till then. Her face was running with sweat, kohl from her eyes streaked her cheeks like smoke. They're still floating there, the bodies. Army left them. Flood'll take them away. She rocked forward, holding out the tattered umbrella. Help me now.

She was coming out into her rain. He raised the umbrella over her as she stood. She was surprisingly tall. Her man-shoulders had rent the dress at its seams. The black fur of her arms held tics, seeds, bits of leaf. Pustules bled there and along her neck. She smiled small at his courtesy and he saw yellow teeth shrunken in dark gums.

She was clawing up her skirt and then her penis was out and a thunderous stream of urine drummed the soil. Atop the grave where she'd forbidden him to stand, foam wheeled and fizzed.

This is not my baby, she said. This is death. Death.

She professed by her piss a disbelief in memory. Nothing but dead are the dead.

Her stance was broad beneath the hiked-up skirt, and to Jude's eyes she straddled a boundary as porous as the soil fizzing underfoot. To her there was nothing so determinate as the death she was pissing down. It was singular. It wanted to divide into singulars all things. But she was no single thing.

# MAN–WOMAN

*They dragged out my wife and shot her in the yard. I saw from the millpond through the trees. I could do nothing. Too far. Indoors, the baby slept. Why'd they leave the baby? When I reached the house I found her still asleep. She was very new, so small she hardly stirred the cradle. She woke crying and wanted her mother. Cruel, her waking to different life. Hours, she cried. What could I do? She was very hungry but the cows were gunned at pasture weeks before, no milk. I carried her to her mother in the yard, laid her down beside her on bloodied footstones and drew out the breast. Cold. All flesh. Senseless and heavy. But there were dots of milk around the nipple like a necklace of pearls. The gums, pasty dry, began to latch. The pale throat worked. I pumped with my hands that breast, then the other. The flesh sank and held the print of my thumbs. My baby's eyes rolled.*

*Soon our neighbor was there. They mean to kill us all, he said, go, go. He hurried up the road. There was gunfire in the village, tight rifle reports, silence. Firing squad.*

*I gathered up what time allowed though we hadn't much of anything left. Then to the forest.*

*Once drunk of my dead wife the baby would not suckle more. We slept in the ferns, the weather. Trees clubbed each other above us.*

*She died with the leaves wadded in her mouth. She bloomed green but that was false spring. The rest of her was winter and no thaw.*

*Death has no other names. It is itself only. It is not starvation that kills. Guns clubs war — these are not death but names we use in its place.*

*From the shrine there are four directions of trail. They seem to go different ways but walk them as I've learned to do and you see the shrine stands centerwise at the crossing of a figure-eight.*

*Out and back, out and back, the shrine is always there.*

*But the eight is imperfect, lopsided, too large on one side. Whoever it was first set the course made a poor job of it.*

. . .

Jude came down into the man-woman's empty village.

In the hollowed streets lay a stillness deeper than abandonment, worse. There was not a great amount of wreckage. The glass remained intact in many windows and he saw but two or three walls demolished to heaps of plaster. But in every house the doors stood open.

There were no birds at the eaves, no dogs in the lanes.

Quietly, methodically, he looked in at each door. Clocks ticked, chimed the hour. Tables stood with chairs pushed in, dinner cloths laid.


In a few hours' foraging he'd filled his sash with provisions. There was more of use here than he could ever carry out. Food was of course scarce but he'd found two potatoes, a dried corncob he would boil for tea, a few ounces of rice, some chunks of bread, an apple core, and — most wondrous — a crust of lemon cake. These and his other oddments he carried along the ghostly streets toward the village's edge.

Passing over a low hill, he saw for the first time a large city hall or church enthroned atop a prominence out beyond the rooftops. There were windows along its ramparts, a copper-crowned bell tower.

There could be anyone up there, with a vantage of all but the smallest streets.

He pressed nearer the walls of the houses, quickening his pace.

After a time the houses dropped away and he was walking a country road in the open. He tried not to think of the all-seeing bell tower at his back. Yet every few minutes his mind would show him the sinister metal eye of a sniper's gun.

There were always these times that called you out past protection. You walked in danger. You sped the bullet on if it was coming.

Breathe, accept the ease of endings, keep walking.


The road curved and ran up another little rise overlooking a marshy pond. Here Jude was hit powerfully by the stench. Then he saw the logjammed bodies bloated in the reeds. A hundred or more, face up, face down, some were naked, blue, cleaved rumps extruding amid algae.

Mats of hair hid the faces of women and young daughters.

Old men sprawled, bellies to the sun.

Above the cluttered water flies were storming.

Jude had lurched to the far side of the road cupping hands to mouth, stumbling on, retching.

Of the men, whose straight razor did he carry in his bundled cloth?

Which of the women had baked the lemon cake?

. . .

Between fields the road ran onward with a long gray
wall to each side, then curved again amid meadows
traced over in running brooks, further walls,
hedgerows.

Enormous white oaks commanded the clearings,
their feet submerged in shadowed pools of grass.
Poplars and waxy-leaved bushels opened around the
peripheries.

Jude saw the skeleton of a horse asleep on its side in
a bed of leaves.


He came to a charred meadow and found a windmill,
blackened. On the shaft the jagged sails turned
listlessly. Below them lay the tinder they'd molted off in
fire.

The windmill door stood open. Dirt floor, the ashy
remains of a wheelbarrow, a collapsed workbench.
Smelled of a chimney inside. But he arranged himself on
the ground just within the door and decided he'd stay
the night, keep the abandoned village at hand. There
would be more to find there and he needed rest,
supplies, before going on — he would come to dryer
country in a few days.

Maybe he'd stay here two nights if nothing in the
village made him think better.

He lay back on dirt floor and the doorposts framed
the day out of darkness, the ruined sails drifting
through the picture.

The turning shaft sang a weak high note, and cooled cinders rustled at his ears.

He was seeing bodies again — the ones in the pond, others. They all looked much the same, as did the moment of their death, whoever must answer for that.


They hadn't clung to many scruples, Jude and the men. The resistance demanded action. You let yourself go. It is necessary. They often left the bodies where they lay. It was a manner of communicating to the aggressors, and to their collaborators. More than once they dragged the bodies about, configuring the double-diamond of the resistance, their insignia. With explosives they blasted trains and roadways, churches, public markets.

One night, sprinting through moon-strafed forest, a mangled train afire behind him, Jude had nearly fallen over a young woman dragging herself arm by arm across the forest floor. The detonation had thrown her clear over his head. Her eyes glowed to watch him pass. She wasn't screaming yet. The stumps of her hips were smoking brands.

Jude remembered more much the same. He was not yet back inside himself. No, that seemed unlikely ever to happen now. Even his name was no help in bridging the chasm. *Jude.* It was of course not his real name. And Dobo, Finn, even X — the war had renamed them all.

.   .   .

*Josepha, though, he had never harmed.*

*He saw her naked breasts slathered with his blood. Her hand letting go of the knife. You should kill me now, she'd instructed him. You can never trust me after this. Instead, he let her wash and bandage the place her knife had entered him.*

*To kill her would be to kill the world. He'd never even considered it.*


On his back in the daylit door of the windmill, Jude unfolded the old woman's Bible page. The slow sails slashed the words with shadows.

> If a man have two wives, one beloved and
> another hated, and they have borne him
> children, both the beloved and the hated,
> and if the firstborn son be hers that was
> hated: Then it shall be, when he maketh
> his sons to inherit that which he hath,
> that he may not make the son of the
> beloved firstborn before the son of the
> hated, which is indeed the firstborn: But
> he shall acknowledge the son of the hated
> *for* the firstborn by giving him a double
> portion of all that he hath: for he *is* the
> beginning of his strength; the right of the
> firstborn *is* his.

Here Jude turned over the page.

If a man have a stubborn and rebellious
son, which will not obey the voice of his
father, or the voice of his mother, and
that, when they have chastened him, will
not hearken unto them: then shall his
father and his mother lay hold on him,
and bring him out unto the elders of his
city, and unto the gate of his place; And
they shall say unto the elders of his city,
This our son is stubborn and rebellious,
he will not obey our voice. And all the
men of his city shall stone him with
stones, that he die: so shalt thou put evil
away from among you.

    Jude laid the paper by.
    He slept in the sweep of sails, his head in trapezoidal
sunlight, his body in darkness. His eyelids were warm
and the canvas of sleep a bluish pink.


X was there. They were sitting in the windmill door.
    X was talking while blood spurted out the spout
between his eyes.
    The blood ran down into his mouth. His lips were
mountains and the river of blood washed over them.
    There were bones in the river. Windmills, smoke.
There were fires in the river. The sun was in the river.

The white feet of a horse were pawing at the sun and a long skull emerged smiling, earless, with socketed eyes.

The skeleton horse sprang and splashed and broke apart.

The bones as they twirled clanged music ...

# BALLADEER

*This fellow he laid there asleeping in the door, I couldn't
have seen him but come right close to fetching a boot in his
ear, and methinks him dead-'n-gone being so poorly looking
and lean of cheek, but on that instant up he comes at my noise
as I all but lose my feet the instruments clanging and what
have you. And oh Christendom he has a gun! A friend a
friend I tell him, nothing to fear, a lowly singer's all I am
and never a man has died a what music I make though some
I won't deny it took umbrage at me voice. He settles a little
then, upon looking me over appears satisfied mostly seeing the
instruments, and we sit there out of the sun some, gandering
each other, not a word. But oh this fellow has seen some
things, has the look about him, and you cannot say how old or
young he may be, nor where he hails from, only that he is a
child of war. Well, be there any in a thousand miles who is
not? No, but some like this one have had their hands right in
it. Some have stains to the elbows, some to the shoulders, and
some like this one all over.*

    *I tell him I'm sorry to wake him, to which he says nothing
but only bends a little and scratches above one eye. I tell him I
stayed here a night some days back. That it's a good enough
place and I'll be happy if he sees fit as I do to share it a time.*

    *Again he looks me over.*

Aint a thief, I tell him, except to steal men's ears for a song. And I strum him a phrase or two for good measure, which does the job of changing his eyes a bit — and now I know he can be trusted. Men while plotting do not listen, music can't get in.

Settling back some on one arm he tells me after a moment's thought he'll have a song now if I will play. Well, as I need no better prompting than this — for music is as bread wine and wife to me — I take up the strings and go to it on the little historical "Shadows Aborning" for I am I will tell you partial to the histories and they're wont to leap to mind. I sing:

> The stars all gathered and flung
> The mooncloth rolled or hung
> The silver-spinning sun
> Each cheat and mark our shades

There are but four verses and yet I can avouch how some men seem by their listening to tug and stretch a tune till all its weave-work shows and the threads of every note and word unravel past proper measuring. Well, this poor fellow was such as that. We made a universe of those few moments him and me, the old song between us like stitching.

Oh such a man it must be has brokered some business with life and death. Were you as I am a listener to listeners you too would see it plain. He told me his name after a time that evening. I did not mind it wasn't his true name. The war leaves more nameless than not — fittingly in this fellow. He'd found his way, surely by no lights of his own, through

*corpse yards and death-dealings into the single heart of man.*
*Such things are possible. Even war may mother us, be she*
*damnable cruel.*

    *When I'd done with the tune I looked at him straight.*
    *Be a good man now and toss the gun away.*
    *And he did.*

.  .  .

Twice Jude went back to the dead village, looking through the open houses. The old ballad singer stayed behind at the windmill or wandered the meadows and brooks with his instruments. Now and then his voice carried faintly over the country to whisper ghostlike in the lanes. Jude would bring him back a little something among his findings, in exchange for songs. Their first night encamped together they made a meager fire in the char outside the door and the singer played for hours, one continuous diminuendo. Up behind them rose a galleon moon, parchment yellow. Higher and higher it shrank as they sat, brightening at its zenith to contest the stars.

The singer sang:

> *Some strode through old Saharan sands*
> *Some sank i' the peace-named sea*
> *All sluff their souls o' borrowed life*
> *To wake as men made free.*

Music, the play of the fire, shadows veiling and unveiling their faces, the slow sails turning across the stars. Because they understood each other they did not talk, and Jude was let down to sleep on the paid-out threads of the ballad.

Until on the second night the balladeer, shelling two peanuts Jude had brought him, said, You've killed many men.

Yes.

Jude would answer to it forever now, own that history and let it be known — else to what purpose had they all died? Honor them, wretches. Yes, I slit throats in the dark. He wouldn't forget the give of the neck, so easy, his hand clamped at the mouth because they always gurgled, knees unbuckling in a groan. Had to immobilize them one by one, that was quietest, working our way in. Always in the street at night. For a long time we stymied them with those incursions. By day they did their evils, come dark we made them answer. We were the same, us and them. We wanted only to out-shame each other.

This went on a long time?

Years. From the earliest start of the war.

And then you were betrayed.

Yes.

Are you angry?

No.

When you first learned of the betrayal, were you angry then?

No.

Are you still a killer, now?

Yes. Because there's no changing what's done. But that is not all I am, I am more than that now. I will never again, you see, be one single thing. And I'm done with killing.

But your countrymen. Have you abandoned them?

No. They are everywhere.

Everywhere?

Everywhere. Yes.

Even those what may gun you down tomorrow?

Yes, sadly even those. And you, Singer?

The balladeer had taken up his strings again. His fingers chorded, stopped, ran a little trill. Oh me, I'm like yourself. What have you when everyone you loved is dead? What have you but the world?

He began to sing.

In the rooms of the houses Jude walked quietly, a
visitor, though his hosts be absent.

Or maybe he was a ghost haunting some old reality,
time before their births.

He knew where the bodies had gone and yet it
seemed, somehow, he caused each room to empty as he
came. His presence rippled. Waves rolled before him to
clear the spaces. The thought taunted and disturbed
him. As if he could get ahead of his presence some way,
jump out of or over his own motion, and overtake the
receding dead. As if he might alight on the parlor
carpet right in their midst. Find them pouring tea,
poking the fire, drawing the housecat into a lap to pet
it.

As it was, daylight streamed through windows and
over furniture to spark in mirrors and brighten corners,
pretending itself needful.

There were children's toys on the hearthrugs, house-
shoes at the foot of the stairs.

Cheekwise on a side table lay a man's pipe, crumbs of
black dottle from the bowl.

Every pantry was bare, all cupboard doors flung,
drawers tilted out. Otherwise the whole village stood in
suspension, a domiciliary holding of breath, a kind of
peace.

It would be days, weeks, before the flowers in the windowboxes began to wilt.

The refugees, the deserters — gypsies, brigands, and other stragglers — had not yet descended, but they would come, perhaps by turns at first, then in tides. Listen, you could all but hear them, their noise of approach over the land.


Jude climbed the quiet stairwells.

He stood at closets shuffling clothes.

All the vanities were ransacked, jewelry boxes overturned, every mantel absent of candlesticks, silver drawers cleaned out.

The medicine chests had been largely left alone, it proved worth his while to check these. Razors, tweezers, tiny magnifiers, needles and thread, scissors, balms, herbs and tinctures, eye pencils, shoeblack, cakesoap — even, in one, little vials and a hypodermic syringe.

He couldn't know what to carry out and what to leave, unsure how little or much he'd find next door. He would just take all he could hold — he'd found a large pilgrim bag — and discard or replace as he continued his search.

Each new threshold cautioned him, but again and again he met with empty rooms.

He'd traded his boots for a sturdier farmer's pair. His own footfalls, echoing, followed him in the lanes.

In a gabled bedroom high in one house he stretched out on his back, boots overhanging the edge of the bed. The coarse handmade blankets were neatly tucked. There was a tea-rose scent in the pillows.

A strand of a woman's dark hair had caught in the hem of one sham. Long and wavy, undeniable against the white, it seemed itself the picture of a woman asleep. The women he'd known had slept like no other creatures, some style of sleep a man could never fathom. Bedded down in their own hair, their own softness, warm mysteries they somehow hugged beneath their breasts. Sleep had fed their powers in a way he'd never seen in men.

At the window under the chapel-like gable there was a valance, rose-pink, scalloped lace at the edges. He lay a long time watching it lift and settle, lift and settle in the breeze.

His world these several long years had been emptied of breezes, noiseless rooms, these gestures a house will make in silence for those who live there, or for nobody.

He smoothed the bedclothes before he left.

*Josepha had a way of fighting out of her blouses. She didn't understand, at first, that it was his pleasure to undress her. She was not inexperienced, but there were certain important things no one had taught her. He placed her hands and, in silence, showed her how to move them. ...*

The balladeer had gone before the light. Jude woke inside the windmill door, alone. Near the fire's ashy ring, peanut shells lay scattered.

He gathered up his findings, the pilgrim bag. His boots, of course, he'd slept in. He would prefer to travel under cover of night but he was ill at ease to stay here longer. He might have lived here indefinitely given different circumstances, but the war indulged no preferences. He would remember the name of the place. Told himself he'd come back to it, though he couldn't say why he needed to believe this. Everything would change once he'd left. Refugees would arrive. It was never to be the same village. He almost believed he'd lived in it, known it when women carried bread in the streets or stood at each other's gateposts gossiping. Men trudged home from fields and leaned on their elbows out the upper story windows, called to their wives to call reprimands to their children playing rough in the street. He almost forgot the late-coming angel of death he'd been in this place. I'll be back, he told himself, and half believed it. The neverness in leaving a place was more than he wished to consider, though he must have known there would be still other places, other leavings.

He would enter the open country of the plains before the night.

．　．　．

The road was good. He determined to stay on it as long as possible — a luxury he hadn't known for years, for he'd related to roads in terms only of destruction or avoidance, crawling near them to lay mines by dark, or cutting wide around them into brush. The war taught him to look for the empty places in maps, to plot the veering course and stray along margins or out across vacant expanse.

It alarmed him to understand the article of blind faith a road could be. How the armies agreed to believe in them. How, the more each army put itself at the road's mercy, the more profound the road became. Roads made logic and religion of the war. You would die for a road, proudly, if a little betrayed in the end.

It wasn't for the aggressors alone that Jude and the men avoided the roads. The resistance was also hunted by its own Army, which judged them unmannerly for shouldering a separate idea of this war. There were codes, traditions, above all there was lawful duty to country — who were they to criticize by taking up a cause all their own?

Many times Jude and the others had to kill their own countrymen. The slit throats gushed over the familiar uniform. This was necessary. They all wanted the same things, but the war would not permit them to want it differently. To live is to be dedicated, though dedication corrodes. Make peace with this and decide.

.  .  .

Jude walked and the farmer's boots were firm, assuring.
He had food to last him meagerly for two days out. He
wore the large hat from the old woman's house, the
brim unbuttoned and flapping. He'd found an oak limb
in a meadow. Stripped of its bark it made a good staff.

A pilgrim now, he thought of the other pilgrims
these roads had carried. They were old, old roads and
those pilgrims were shadows upon the road, moving in
darkness though it was day. They were uniformed and
steadily walking — but not in column, not in pace.
They didn't look at him as they came but their slit
throats seemed to smile.

He had one of the singer's ballads in his mind. He
started to hum and they joined him, the broken throats
blooming music.

Where would the balladeer go? Who would he sing
to next?


Jude had thrown the gun away this morning. It
splashed in the swamp where the bodies floated. Small
scavenger birds sprang up with flickering wings.


Unlike most others in the resistance, he'd never hated
the Army soldiers. Of course he understood this hate —
how it *helped*, and how for his fellow fighters it was a
kind of healing some days.

Even comrade soldiers entrenched together learn at some level to hate *each other.*

You hate because you want to love, but love is too dangerous.

Jude could not judge the others for hating. But for him it was different.

Once, in the capital city, on a midnight raid of their own Army's hospital, he slipped into a dark ward to walk the long rows of beds where the young casualties slept — or splayed awake — untrousered with their wounds.

He was older than most of them.

They were a sight in their starched white sheets, shadows tucked beneath them in the dark.

The sleeping ones each seemed a child, wholly surrendered to bed, the hospital, the war outside. They were wombed in a dream of kinds. They were men who killed, but the horrors bred of that business resembled nothing so much as old childhood horrors.

When you were small, in the heat of the nursery at midday, worlds gaped, anything could happen — and now, all over again, that strangeness surged back at you. This is why those awake in the dark merely stared as he passed by.

Because they were men they did not cry, but like children they were watching all the time for someone to come and marshal the darkness.

Some did cry, of course. The drugs would release them, their pains and visions, their grief at the body they'd each taken for granted — the arms or legs now gone, the fingers and fucking parts.

Jude stopped at the bed of one who seemed asleep. A boy, he had no legs. His torso consequently had the strangely swollen look of the maimed.

His head on the pillow was small, almost shrunken. A fringe of black hair, straight and high on the brow. Girlish work of a nurse's shears.

Jude, unthinking, bent very close, listening, leaning, till he breathed the sleeper's recitative breath.

# AMPUTEE

*These halls, it's all angels and ghosts. Bits and pieces of world and afterworld mixed up and stirred. Like Mama how she stirred the eggs and the liquid spun in the bowl even after she stopped to tap the spoon. The darkness smells of disinfectant, nurses come and go on soft shoes, the bed stiffly holds me or what's left. They said the mortar threw me ten yards, more. I remember nothing. Training, yes. The barracks. Drill. Nothing of the fight though I'm told I killed a bunch. Those ones never killed me but for payment cut me in half. Aint nothing ever free, like Papa used to say. I don't cry about it like some of these boys but I can't blame them, even the ones in better shape than me. Crying's likely good for a fellow only I've never been myself that kind. Papa used to pound me but didn't ever get the tears to come. Cried when I was small like any other but never after that.*

*Are there pains? Yes, for certain, and a hell of a chore to turn over back to front, can't lay on your side either less you've got a leg to keep you weighted.*

*Worst of it's the sores the bed makes all over. Nurses forget to turn me sometimes but tell the truth I'm amazed they remember as often as they do having their hands plenty full.*

*I could call for them but mostly I don't, I just never was one to complain much.*

*Sleep's not so easy, true, but laying awake in a bed legs or not is nothing to cry for, especially knowing what the men outside in the fight have for comforts. Not anything, is what.*

*I lay and wait, and even sometimes awake as I am, I get in a state a little like sleep.*

*You see things then. Angels, ghosts get up and walk around. They're kindly sorts, and set you to wondering what's all the fussing and fearing over death? This one night they're moving up and down back and forth in the ward, no more than friendly shadows, just gliding, sort of a comfort really — and one somehow gets very close before I see or hear him and bends right down and, just like Papa used to do before I got older and earned his pounding, just like I forgot he ever did for I must have been awful small, this shadow, angel, whatever, bends down and kisses my head just over the eye, very same place as Papa though I forgot it for years.*

*Before I blink wider to look he's gone.*

*The shadows are just shadows again not moving at all.*

. . .

The country ahead of him narrowed. The road passed through a series of short tunnels. Along the stone walls arches let in the light. Jude moved in pools of sun and shadow, passed into open day again.

It was twelve days, more, since he'd murdered X. The war as he'd known it had ended for him there. Now, moving into changing country, he felt the war receding.

The road snaked down along the foothills, then the country opened out on one side to slope away in diminishing folds, drier, browner by degrees until in the distance the plains laid everything smooth, stretching off forever. There was a front in the far north of that country, but it wasn't his war.

He began to see falcons, hawks.

Smaller birds palpitated, silver-shouldered.

The country lay on and on and the daylight in the distant haze above the plains was like a scuffed lens.


In the afternoon the rain began. Jude had left the road and was walking in a clodded field. Soon the ground was puddled and splashing about his feet.

He had an oilcloth he'd taken from the kitchen table in an empty house. He draped it overhead, raising a corner in each hand, felt the runoff coursing along his back. It smelled of butter.

The air steamed and he sweated under his clothes.

Just before twilight he came to stand in a rubbled area. Ruins of houses surrounded him for a square mile or more, such wreckage that nothing stood higher than his knees. He'd been there before, in the war's first year.

He remembered a settlement of clustered earthen houses, neatly geometrical on the edge of the plains. Ages old, the place had been inhabited and deserted many times over, in recent years by the nomadic bands who roamed this low country with their stock.

The Army found it a suitable outpost and staging point, deploying contingents, running intelligence relays, and, in a series of small hovels made to serve for stockade, detaining prisoners.

On one of his first resistance forays Jude had been collared crossing the lines and brought here, where for two months he was held in a windowless room.

The warden was a commander from the village neighboring Jude's, and thanks to this man's fellow-feeling Jude was spared much worse than a few days of roughing up by the guards. These soldiers mishandled him till he bled about the face, then kicked him on the floor, but they were unpersuasive. The anger in their blows told a story other than the happiness of their subservience.

Surprisingly he was never interrogated. The Army saw little cause to take the resistance seriously. The resistance, as far as the Army was concerned, amounted to the acting out of a minor faction. The Army would simply stem these disruptions and absorb that admittedly useful energy into the orthodox force of division, battalion, platoon. It was just a matter of rounding up the fighters — how many could there be? — and pounding the rowdiness out of them.

Neither resistance nor Army could yet foresee the secondary, interior war, the slaughter of compatriots, bound to emerge from their differing visions of how best to slaughter the enemy.

After his second month in prison Jude was made to pledge his rehabilitation. Fitted out in uniform he was given a few weeks' training and, in a convoy of fellow rehabs, carried to meet his new line readying to make a counterattack in the southeast.

He was a week in that force before, on the night of their third day marching, he slipped into the woods. Doubled back through forest to find his men at their meeting place. He nearly scared them into shooting him as he came scuttling Army-clad from the trees.

In the following years Jude wore the uniform of both armies many times on incursions. Caring little for either one, he came to see the oath inherent in his non-uniform too.

.   .   .

Jude sat a time amid the ruins in the rain. There were the first two steps of a stair and they made a kind of seat. Out beyond what were once the limits of the settlement, a few scraggly pine trees swayed, the last remnants of forest before the plains.

To the north, above the open country, a band of paling light lay beneath a sunken ceiling of cloud.

Jude could picture the scene reversed: standing at that horizon looking back over darkening land, his own figure invisible against the layers of hills, the rain like a streak of chalk someone's thumb had made.

Would he see this way forever now? From all directions?

The past could not be kept behind.

Looking at the future, even, was a kind of looking back.

The swaying trees, the great land flowing to the horizon, the churning surf of clouds — being in this was all, and you were in all of it at once.

He got up and started walking again.

There was a whispering in his ears. Something the rain was saying.

# OLD GHOST

*We keep to no one place, my kind, we are several selves. How good to be scattered abroad like seed, how fitting. Your time having come you welcome this, you wonder at the strangeness of a body, its boundaries, that thralldom always. How were you so small? How was it you reckoned the sadness, or failed to see it at all — the constant sadness of maps?*

*We led the herds this way each year. My grandfather's father did the same. I slept upon rooftops here, blanketed in stars, my feet so hard with walking I felt nothing of the night on my toes. I remember no dreams from then, only sleep.*

*Is this the dream?*

*And how is it you come here? Do these ruins surprise? I was here when they wrecked it and the Army was routed. Was it your Army? It wasn't the first. Armies of every size, every purpose have passed this way. All were equal in their seriousness.*

*You look almost like one of us, except that your memories still clothe you. That will change, your time having come. Memories finally fail to cling. They linger around and underfoot, like the land itself, but they do not shape you. You will have no shape, and this, you will understand, is natural, more natural than living.*

*I too did not know how it would be in this aftertime. We
had our gods and prayers and they were helpful in their way.
In those we loved and understood each other and did not feel
so very alone, even in our inescapable bodies. Giving us
marriage, religion gave us entry into bodies not our own. My
wife and I on our wedding night unlocked one another —
before that you cannot know in what yearning life passes.
Outward into the other, wife and I caught glimpse of this
being-everywhere, this world-as-memory. How everything,
every action, is part of the search for this.*

*Oh, but you forget in time. We did. Gods and prayers are
helpful, but these things you cannot live and remember, not
while rooted in time where memory clings.*

*And I wouldn't wish you or anyone to be spared the
anxious singularities of life — those have their purpose.*

*But I see you've caught scent of something here. I see
you've entered armies like bodies. I thought despite your close-
fitting tunic of memory you might understand.*

*Do you understand?*

.   .   .

Jude tried the syringe. Couldn't be much harm using one vial, and he wanted whatever help he could get crossing over the plains. The prospect of gravity, of his every step pinning him in that expanse, of being small and constrained amid the outspreading force of the land — this made him wish for numbness, oblivion, a dream to contract his limitless thought.

The needle dug. A teardrop of blood ran from the hinge of his arm toward the wrist. Under his thumb the plunger fell. Then came a cold stream from the vial.

He walked in total dark.

The dark sponged up rain, clouds, sky.

His feet fell silently but he was breathing, breathing, and his clothes rustled.

The black land was a belt moving beneath him. He felt if he stopped he'd stream backward on his feet.

He was entirely inside his own body, an eye that had closed.

Someone had strung a thread of white across the black before him, razor's trail across the neck of dark, and now the slit throat was bulging forth an egg, gleaming, bulb-white. Growing, it trailed a skirt of splendor and he walked under the high receding sun, the table underfoot upended, spinning, till he smashed his head on air. And his head broke apart to splinter about his shoulders with the clangor of sprung strings.

His head was the broken instrument of the ballad singer. The strings were only wires now. They shuddered, reverberatory, and died.

Have some sense, said the commander.

Jude was brought beaten and handcuffed to the man's quarters.

The commander's uniform was very crisp, creases of sleeves and trousers so sharp they looked drawn on. He stood by the corner of his massive desk, which was of darkly lacquered wood and embellished down the sides with arabesques, angel faces each no bigger than a man's thumb. The desk filled half the room. Jude couldn't see how it ever came to be in the room, for here as in all the clay houses the door was squat and narrow.

What is this 'resistance'? said the commander. Resistance is a word. You wish to die for a word?

Army, too, was a word. But Jude made no answer.

The commander bent to consult the silver coffee service a subordinate had placed at one side of the desk.

The gem of a large forefinger ring glimmered darkly.

Steam leaked from a serpentine spout. Black stuff burbled into two fluted glasses. The commander presented one of these to Jude where he sat in the straight wooden chair. Manacled, Jude drank with both hands, the coffee a scalding medicine.

We are neighbors, you and I, said the commander, whose ring looked very decorous against the crystalline rim of his glass. He seemed to want to pace before the desk, to make the most of his jodhpurs and polished boots, but the indigenous dimensions of the room forbade this dignity, so he merely leaned a little on one hand. Neighbors look after each other's interests, he said. If you noticed me building my barn too near the cutbank, you would warn me. Just as I, seeing you plotting your foundation over a sinkhole, must help you survey a better site.

Pleased with the power of analogy he sipped thoughtfully. He blotted his mustache on the back of his hand.

Jude was cupping the glass in his palms, the deep heat of the coffee. The last coffee he'd drunk was six months before, in a stone kitchen where bread was baking.

*Josepha stooping, oven mitts to her elbows, bringing out a tray. Umberto the baker's daughter.*

*She lived in the wrong place, had stakes in the wrong movement.*

*Kiss her, though, and you cannot think of sectors.*

*Eat bread from her hand and there is no more ideology.*

You and I are born of the same country, the commander continued. We started as equals, as brothers. I was no one, like you, I was nothing. I was happy to have potatoes to boil, a door to shut snug, a fire in my hearth, even if it smoked. I was... He let out a little piff of air and the ringed hand swept before him. Nothing. But you see what's happened now. I was *faithful*, and faith like mine is rewarded. What were you, what are you now? You've told yourself a story all this time, and the story has misled you — that there can be two wars, more. No. There is only one war. You and your comrades will fight it my way. There is no other way.

The commander's voice was low. He was shaking his head, regretful on Jude's behalf.

He was not gloating, only observing an unfortunate truth. He spread his hands.

You might have been in a position like mine by now, there's no reason not. This, however, is no longer possible. Of course you know this. A man is given his chance. He takes it or he doesn't. He fights for something or for nothing. But let me ask you, and I mean this quite seriously, I want to know: What did you think you stood to gain?

But of course the question was framed in a way that showed he expected no answer.


*Josepha: There's no winning this, you know. Not your way.*
*She was touching him, her tongue at the back of his ear.*
*He shrugged a little. Then we'll lose — but happily. We'll know we tried. He urged her down on the pillows, found the golden arch of her midriff under the hem of her blouse. There's no such thing anyway. Winners. We know this, don't we, Jo? They don't exist.*

*No, she answered.*

*Meaning what, exactly? He would not ask, for he was down now and kissing her, and her moans were music.*

The prisoner was returned to his cell and further beaten.

Jude woke to the glaring pressure of sun on his lids.

Blinking, blinded, he found himself heaped on the ground, his clothing soaked heavy as a hide. He'd walked all night in the rain.

A wind was stirring. It came across that vast vacancy behind him, trembling the water puddled everywhere. He shivered.

Digging in his pilgrim sack: the clothes inside, though wet, seemed only damp compared to those he wore. He stood up to skin himself of shirt, overshirt, trousers.

Naked in combing wind, in the privacy of that vast openness on the plains, he stretched his hands high. He jumped twice and felt the sink of the clay under the balls of his feet.

Unmoving earth, absolute.

If only he could plant himself there, treelike, and without moving, grow. ...

Ahead in the middle distance the land began to ripple, rising into a low haze beyond which stood a verdant wall of hills.

He shook his drenched clothes, then wrung them overhead, catching the musty water in the open cup of his mouth.

# COMMANDER

*What can you say about some men? Some men are like strays. They need mange in their coats or they are unhappy. A man of this kind may be starving and still believe he is free.*

. . .

# 2.

# Works Lost:
## the Private Papers
## of G.P. Leed

"Who is there lives for beauty? Still am I /
the torch, but where's the moth that still dares die?"

—Arthur Symons, *Images of Good and Evil*

*The following extracts are from notebooks kept in my 53rd year. It is my wish that this material, if ever it is discovered, be published together with "In Country," in the order of arrangement I have specified, as a secondary part to that work.*—G.P.L.

In this room there's a small bookcase with narrow doors of glass. An antique, I think. It was here when I settled in. My few books are arranged inside it, happily so. As there is no mirror to be found, I make use of the bookcase doors if ever I need to look at myself. I like the faintness of the image reflected back at me. The spines of the books are much bolder, as seems only fitting.

*

The fear of beginning a new work. This is actually nothing other than the fear of <u>finishing</u>. Of, ultimately, death. That dear horror of the firmly decided, the complete and conclusive: without this there is no art.

*

A man heaves a tool and strikes the earth, the better to master the little plot he stands upon. The earth at large does not flinch.

*

Say to yourself: There will be no rewards. Don't look around, don't review your past, your wasted hours, the life that led to your loneliness and folly. At this moment the world must not exist. There is no world except as you make it. Be at peace with this, sit down, work.

*

It's begun. Already the taint is on it. Nevertheless I have started.

*I had begun work on a new book, referred to elsewhere in my notes by the title "The Partisan." I would later change this to "In Country."*—G.P.L.

*

A short unlikely chat with the Doctor today, in passing, about a few of the framed prints he keeps hung in the stairwell — Whistler's "Nocturne in Blue-Green," Van Gogh's "The Ox-Cart," a few Cezannes. "I've always loved them," he told me. "Who cares if they're Irrelevant. At one time anyway they were valuable. They meant something. I suppose I live a little in the past, but I don't mind." And he gave me, sidelong, that shy look of understanding, of sympathetic appreciation silently conveyed, that I've come to expect from him despite his reticence. He can be trusted, I have no doubt. And without in the least seeming to compromise this trustworthiness, he indicates quite clearly that he has no intention of being an ally in a proactive sense. Still, his wing is open and I crawl under. For a time anyway. Up here we are forty miles shy of the national border, and out my window lies the view toward British Columbia, a sea of imbricate evergreens.

*Leed was letting a small room in the attic of a retired doctor in Bellingham, Northwest Territory. The sea of evergreens would feature frequently in his writing.—Ed.*

*

The Doctor is a shy one. Not mousy, just retiring. Speaks in a semi-whisper so you feel the need to lean closer, tune yourself down. This morning he brought up a potted fern, said he believes in keeping the house well stocked with plant life. Oxygenating properties, etc.

I thought my ways were quiet enough, but I worry I'll become a nuisance to such a man. My typewriter rings like thunder through walls and floor.

*

One's youth is passed much in the homes of others — an experience we lose as time goes on. We simply pay more visits when we're young. To be an adult is to be cooped up within mind and self, and it seems to me we need a term, a single descriptive word, to capture the sore-at-heart longing for that early variety. The word "nostalgia" doesn't cut close enough. No, the yearning I mean is concerned with a very specific narrowing, an impoverishment in one's experience of the domicile. As you get older, you lose hold of the sense of a generalized hearth, a world of comforts and welcomes, the simple stimulus of eating at another family's table. You begin to believe, in a sense, that adulthood has overtaken everything, that all families have been scattered from their tables, that the grown-up world is the only world there is, and that it is a world of a hundred billion singulars, a hundred billion lonely ex-

77

children exiled from the creature comforts of a pre-established home. Your own world gets austere and ascetic, limited to three or four rooms, a stairwell perhaps, the static proscenia of a few windows — and this you take to be indicative of life for everyone.

Oh for a friend's mother and a cup of milk from her kitchen.

*

My quarters

*

The Doctor receives no visitors. Sometimes the house is silent half the day and I assume he's gone out, then I pass him on the landing and it's clear he's been in all morning. I've yet to see him sitting at the kitchen table or sleeping in an easy chair. He does not lounge in the parlor.

Yesterday, hearing voices below my window, I looked out to find him in conversation with a neighbor while watering the lawn. He's lived in this house 53 years, the length of my lifetime. His wife died 15 or 16 years ago. All his neighbors are a great deal younger than him. They patronize him kindly, as young people will do.

*

To Cedric's this afternoon, in Cedric's absence as it turned out. Kasden is staying there, charged to look after the place while Cedric is away on honeymoon. It does need looking after, such a house. Not knowing Cedric well, I'd never visited before, and Kasden saw my surprise the minute I stepped inside. "I know, I know," he said. "I can't begin to tell you how he pays for it." In the course of my visit we walked from room to room, largely to take stock of Cedric's vast book collection, which sprawls upstairs and down. In his study on the second floor we stood at his desk, which he's placed with a view out the front window. There were notebooks, notecards, and piles of printed looseleaf everywhere. Cedric is writing a novel, though this fact is all Kasden knows of the work. "It can't be easy," Kasden said. "Editing eats up so much time." Kasden himself was Cedric's colleague at *Green Window* for a number of years, until Kasden's censure by the Bureau two or three years ago, at which point the *Green Window* editorial board asked him to resign. "I'm a liability," he told me at the time. "The Bureau can't tell anybody who to hire or fire, but if *Green Window* keeps me on they're looking at serious pressure — monthly editorial audits, restricted circulation, loss of ad revenue, and of course a steady attack on their M.V.R. They know this, I know it, so I'll take the fall. It's only right. I have no desire to sabotage the magazine." Since then, Kasden's been freelance editing, scraping things together, just keeping afloat. Because his editorial standards and proclivities haven't changed, he's basically on the lam. And now, since he's already classified as a renegade anyway, he's cooking up a scheme to enter the book trade. He tells me he's in dialogue with various contacts, predicts he'll secure a location within the year. "I'll sell your books," he says with a smile, slapping my shoulder. "Maybe after a while I'll even print them!" He'll have to, I say. How else will they see the light of day?

*Green Window: this magazine, revered in its time, was among the last of the avant-garde print periodicals. / M.V.R.: Market Viability Rating, the chief metric utilized by the Market Optimization Bureau in determining which literary works may be promoted and sold.—Ed.*

*

"We go our own ways," says Kasden, perched on the arm of the sofa in Cedric's upstairs study. "We work in the dark, we do what we can, and there's no helping how things turn out."

But he sees I find this hard to accept.

"Look," he says, "the work doesn't change. You put

something down in words, you stay with it, you try to tell the truth. Whatever happens afterwards, that part doesn't change. Times are hard, sure, and harder for some than others. So..." He shrugs. "You go your own way."

The study is hot and bright with upstairs sun. Surrounding us, Cedric's books in their printed jackets seem to grow more and more colorful, the lenses of Kasden's glasses gleam strangely, his hands saw the air.

*

I remember, many years ago, hearing a singer's voice through a wall. A neighbor girl, a musician. Tentatively she would work through a new composition, or sometimes in full voice she'd sing a long-finished piece. I got to know those melodies, some of the words even. And later, after a few years, having moved my residence, I began to hear the same melodies on the radio, in shops, blaring from passing cars. Realizing I'd known that music when it was still just the private business of a girl singing haltingly in a room.

*

On the 12th-century cathedral at Autun, west of Dijon, on the stonework lintel above the main door, you find the chiseled words: "Giselebertus Made This." The first of its kind, this determined signature in an age of anonymity. The seizure of an identity from the Cult of Carts. Is this vanity? Above the words: a carved tympanum of the Last Judgment, Christ's arms spread wide in majesty.

And there's a story that tells of Michelangelo

stealing by night into the great basilica in Rome, chisel and hammer in hand, to inscribe his name below the hem of his *Pieta*'s sad Madonna.

Vanity? No, these names were not about the glory of the artist. They were about the act of creation in a brutal age. A signature was a refusal to be disowned by one's epoch, to have one's gift refused. It was an act of rebellious generosity of spirit. We will not be anonymized. We will not be robbed of our power to give. Giving is our destiny!

*

Remembering, years ago — a lifetime back — sitting in a corridor inside a great city's museum (London, Paris, Vienna?), and looking into the elegant little museum restaurant at the many people happily dining in there. They were my countrymen, a number of them. I wonder if I can adequately touch upon what I saw happening amongst these people, of the way they formed a collective. Can I convey how, for me, they all seemed to become knitted together in comfort and enjoyment, in a conscious understanding of their own enrichment? No doubt many of them were fine and discerning individuals — but epoch and geography, the moment's context, lay like a warping glass over the scene and fused its colors. For naturally I was young and quite poor: I could not go inside and order anything.

All this eating and enjoyment transpired in front of the huge daylit nimbus of the clock's face on the museum's façade. They were inside the clock and were very small together. The clock's black roman numerals, each as tall as a man, hung reversed against blue sky, and every minute the gigantic hand swept soundlessly through another notch in the day.

In the crowded galleries around us hung works made in mad private devotion, works born arduously in solitary rooms or out of doors on the loneliest easels, works received in their own time with public revulsion. And what looked frightful, here on this day, what seemed so hard to accept, was the manner in which these same works were now being *claimed*. Claimed, owned, and made the subject of cultured lunchtime talk.

Did I perceive then the beginning of all that has happened since? Maybe, but I could predict nothing of the extent to which this 'ownership' could go, and in so short a period, my own lifetime. How those works of art, the ones that were not destroyed, anyway, could be made in a matter of a few decades the exclusive property of the elites, reduced to decoration and thus rendered Irrelevant.

And what one still finds frightful, so very hard to accept, is how this appropriation all but strips those bygone artists of the only thing that was ever truly, consistently theirs. I mean of course their poverty, their obscurity, the painful solitude that gave rise to the works. This was the most they ever had, in the end, and it was something intensely valuable to the artists who would follow. It was a gift for generations. Ownership takes the gift away.

*

Daily we hear it said that history is over, that all is future now. The only reasonable response to this is to set about the work of remembering. One owes it to oneself, if not to the unknown numbers of persons in one's same position, to pause and formulate in one's own words the nature of the situation. So, for whomever may find this after my death, at the earliest beginning of the long-forestalled reconstruction, here is what we gave up (I may as well number them):

1) <u>History</u>. It was said that looking to the earthly past never saved us from repeating mistakes and

perpetuating folly, and never produced much beyond sentimentalism, guilt, nostalgia — all liabilities to progress. Today everything is future.

2) <u>Democracy</u>. An unduly prolonged experiment yielding discord and gridlock.

3) <u>Socialist Democracy</u>. A form of status quo stagnation, overly concerned with legislation, regulation, and security. (Technocracy alone is held to be truly future-oriented.)

4) <u>Civic Aspiration</u>. Because the Network and the digital citadel it promises is an end far superior to 'temporal improvements' in the physical confines of any single locale.

5) <u>Analog Media</u>. Because of course a) these cannot be Market-Optimized, and b) the value of all cultural production is endowed by the Network.

6) <u>Print</u>. (An analog medium, but considering its peculiarly authoritative character, it deserves a classification of its own.) Paper, being un-Networkable, is designated Irrelevant and wherever possible (i.e., while respecting property rights) subject to Processing: recycled into fiber for clothing and Network optic cables. Aforementioned property rights have presented only negligible impediments to large-scale Processing; people happily abandon the physical encumbrance of paper for the supra-physical cleanliness and ease of digital text.

7) <u>Free Production</u>. The Network controls all production. All power or cultural influence hinges upon access to the Networked marketplace, and everything is

monitored. While the Network is purportedly "open to all," in truth what obtains there is a commercial hierarchy of the most entrenched and relentless kind. One's M.V.R. is one's scarlet letter, predetermining rank or lack thereof.

We have seen the deliberate draining away of significance from the works and traditions of Western Civilization. This due to the abandonment of historical perspective and the total supersession of individualism as a cultural value. Furthermore, the Network's effect of undermining civic aspiration — that age-old emphasis on the importance of municipal, civilizational centers of knowledge and human achievement — has led to the loss of an infrastructure that is anything more than barely functional.

Futurity, Collectivity, Technology (social, interactive, virtual, interplanetary), the Network, Objectivity, Plutocratic Aspiration, Market Optimization — these are the ultimate values and aims of the age. All things serve these or perish in Irrelevance.

*

There. It is useful to think over all that has happened. It clears the head. I am Irrelevance embodied.

*

"But his love of the word kept growing sweeter and sweeter, and his love of form; for he used to say (and had already said it in writing) that knowledge of the soul would unfailingly make us melancholy if the

*86*

pleasures of expression did not keep us alert and of good cheer." — T. Mann
*T. Mann: Reference unknown.—Ed.*

*

Often in old photographs from artist colonies or literary conferences you would see a caption something like: "Bottom row, left: unidentified man." What is it, to become a mystery in an old photograph (or not even as much as a mystery)? Only this, maybe: to be dematerialized into the holy privacy of one's day-to-day labors. To let the indescribable, unshareable process swallow you up. What is fame, what is posterity, compared to the secret irrevocable glory of having had one's work?

*

Or do I write such things merely because I suspect that I, by no choice of my own, am bound to disappear?

*

"I am very cold without fire or covering ... the robin is singing gloriously but though its red breast is beautiful I am all alone. Oh God be gracious to my soul and grant me a better handwriting." —Anonymous scribe, medieval Ireland

*

Yesterday while crossing the park, I passed a man with jowls as loose and pendulous as a winded dog's. At first he looked unremarkable beyond his slightly disheveled jacket and shirt. But as he came closer I saw the white beaded strings of slaver swaying from his unfurled bottom lip. He brushed past me with a glazed stare at

*87*

the grass, a stare that might — to someone not looking closely — appear pensive.

*

And then on the sidewalk, the brawny balding man flat on his back and unconscious. He lay in front of the iron gates to that bright yellow house that always reminds me of a guidebook photo. The man was not sidled up to the building or the gate, like most of them, but sprawled across the pavement in a bodily X, as if fallen from some unthinkable height. I actually looked up. It was raining. Did I say that yet? The rain fell on his face, his clothes, his outflung hands, and he didn't move.

*

The crooked man too. He was at the corner, his upper body wildly disfigured to the shape of a crescent moon. He was in the rain, coatless, pacing. He kept turning and turning on mincing feet, two steps this way, two that way. He looked confused and was clearly in agony. Every little motion cost him dearly, his pain ensnared him, but he kept changing direction as if thinking he'd found an escape and then remembering there was none.

*

They are everywhere, of course, once you go out. Whomever is healthy and protected stays indoors. But the sidewalks teem with them, these figures forgotten by the Network.

*

Of course, earthly and civic disrepair are unimportant, for technology, if it does not soon enough enable the 'stabilization of environments' (oxygenized, climate-

*88*

proof structures, etc.), will deliver us to a new planet and fresh futurity. We have become a people for whom 'field' means a white space on a screen, awaiting input of data.

*

"The political awareness that is not aware, the social consciousness which hates full consciousness, the moral earnestness which is moral luxury." —Trilling
*Trilling: reference unknown.—Ed.*

*

An aristocrat in the Republic of Venice was subject to rules so rigid that even his clothing was prescribed. When moneyless nobles took to the streets to beg, they would do so in silken raiment.

*

The way a limp is a story.

*

The strange, lovely way in which, at a wedding, the bride is everybody's bride. The collective wish to protect and cherish her. The vulnerability of the white dress.

*

The way a girl's shoulders will fall when trying to remember a word and failing.

*

Bats under the bridge. To be above a creature flying, to look down at the working wings instead of up, and remember how partial, how piecemeal is one's grasp of the world.

*

The mystery of water burbling from Parisian, Roman, or Turkish taps. Out of what ancient municipal cisterns? Carrying what nourishing and putrefying history?

*

I've reached an impasse with *The Partisan*, temporary I hope.

Still, the longer I sit with them, the pages acquire secrets. A good thing. You work for this always, you want the pages to know more than you do. That way, they can lead you. The struggle for control, the doubt about a thing's direction, the sense of manipulating the material, all that awkwardness goes away. You are free because the work is free. You merely give yourself up to its pull. Your task is to listen and let go. I am on the brink of this. The important thing now is to wait — but to wait in the most active way possible. To remain in attendance. To keep myself available. "Being inactive with confidence," Rilke called this.
*Rilke: unknown personage.—Ed.*

*

There is no state of abiding purity, only the workman's pure concern.

No quality of arrival, only the labor of arriving at.

No reposing in the spirit of a thing, only inspired tenacity — a vision for climbing toward, clawing after, catching onto.

"Should come as naturally as leaves to a tree, or it shouldn't come at all." How impoverished literature would be, how damned and troubled every poor scribbler, if we took such an edict to heart.

*Should come as naturally: Leed seems to be quoting a literary voice. Reference unknown.—Ed.*

\*

"A sort of beautiful sacrifice to a noble mistake." I discovered this phrase today in Henry James — a reference to the career of a third-rate sculptor he knew. What a sentiment! From time to time, one will of course ask of oneself, Do I waste my life? But *Beauty, Nobility, Sacrifice* — may these be the overriding qualities.

*Henry James: American author born sometime in the mid 19th-century. Most of his corpus, though it may still be found with moderate ease, goes unread.—Ed.*

\*

A note today from Kasden. He has secured a space and is busy setting up shop. I must pay him a visit.

\*

Night before last — no, three nights ago — dreamt I'd gone to an artist colony. The place was crawling with grizzly bears, strange because the setting was garden-like. But every walk outside meant a possible encounter, the dread of imminent peril. There were many confusing paths. A great lake, and one was always marooned on the far side, late for the communal dinner, with a view of the main house across the water, its dining room window aglow. There was a vast parking lot and you walked in confusion amid a sea of cars. You were always hungry and had to sneak food from the kitchen, but kept getting caught by your fellow artists, who sneered and harangued.

*

Very soon after awaking and recalling that dream, I remembered the childhood mystery of nights in the quiet hours before sleep, a cheek to the pillow, and the peculiar, measured crunch of marching feet: imagined militia men tromping up and down the hall just beyond the bedroom door.

Only well into adulthood, thinking back to these early vivid sleepheavy impressions, did I ever come to the logical conclusion. It was always my pulse I heard. Falling asleep, soothed and confused, to the march of my own heart.

How little has changed.

*Almost nothing is known of Leed's childhood. This entry is one of a mere handful that vaguely allude to that period of his life.—Ed.*

*

I may sublimate my discontents, but this sitting alone in a room, this being damned to one's papers and desk, this never-ending crawl toward a light that shines nowhere but in one's mind, this condition of divorce from one's world and fellow men — this, when I am calm and quiet and wholly in the groove, is a condition I embrace happily and naturally. When I am in it I know, then I know beyond the doubt, bitterness, loneliness, and privation of my other moments, that this is life to me, and that only in this way can I ever hope to

be a member of the greater world and brother to its
women and men.

*The above was one of the first of Leed's entries to be uploaded
by Market Optimization Bureau agents, and with the
writings that followed there was little difficulty proving him
in breach of the Program for Economic and Objective Purity
in Literary Enterprise (P.E.O.P.L.E).—Ed.*

*

"To seek the anonymous is thought to be inhuman. But
it is in the anonymous that we discover all we share and
therefore what is profoundly human." —Janos Lavin
*Janos Lavin: unknown personage.—Ed.*

*

Dear Kasden,
How long has it been since I sat to write you a proper
letter? Well, there is always the matter of fighting off
self-consciousness, of forgetting the anachronism one
has become (we're both anachronisms, God knows), and
of sitting down to tradition. For there's a quality of
time-honored ritual in any good letter — despite the
overthrow of epistolary form by instantaneous
transmission. There's a state of mind one wants to get
into, a tone of relaxed thoughtfulness that is something
like conversation (although it is actually monologue), a
quality of voice suggesting free and easy expression,
finesse, felicity, flow. The best kind of letter is a gift, an
act of meticulous generosity deployed disguised as a jot,
a fraternal toss-off. Painstakingly constructed, its effect
consists of seeming organic. What a curious form, and
how beautiful. Oh, but letters are losing. Or they lost,

like you and me, a long time ago. And yet, here's a thing I've always admired you for, Kas: being outmoded or outranked has never fazed you. You've got a way of taking circumstances in stride. Me, on the other hand, I can never seem to shake the suspicion that all is arrayed against me, as if somewhere just beyond the light sit clucking rows of spectators awaiting my fall. (Egotism, my God!) No wonder writers are driven to work as we do. For literature, in the absolute submission it requires, eats away at the ego, and how we need this, the lot of us. Or to move to metaphor of another kind, we waddle and whittle and push together dam after dam and our beaver teeth never grow too long. There's a great deal more to it all, of course, than these questions of self-interest or self-abnegation. The dams themselves come to mean everything, the shaping and fitting together of the sticks for the pure purposes of harmony and sound construction. The offering, finally, of the harmonious and soundly constructed to others. Yes, and this energy that is ever mounting toward an externalized, aesthetic, hopefully meaningful structure — this energy has its roots in the ego's dread conviction of selection, of being picked out for damnation of a kind, and of the primordial self-preserving reflex. We writers are good puritans. We know the devil to be everywhere, we are always in heathen country, the infidels beyond the village would kill us in a heartbeat. But by contrast, Kas, how unencumbered you are. How native your freedom. To lose your *Green Window* position despite your labors, to suffer the Bureau's attentions, it is what it is and signals no conspiracy against you. I remember you walking into the tobacco shop that day some time ago, having decided to learn to smoke a pipe. You went in there knowing nothing and I watched you place yourself entirely at the mercy of the shop's old know-it-all proprietor whose chief joy in life was to safeguard his arcane tradition and the air of capable wisdom it lent him and to talk down to non-initiates like you and me. Well, you just <u>listened</u> to the bastard. You engaged and eventually charmed him and an hour later when we walked away you'd won your little nugget of knowledge. Pipestem in mouth, vanilla-scented clouds pluming, you couldn't have been more content. Me, I've never stood up well in such situations. I hate to have anything lorded over me and I detest anybody who will reduce a person merely for wishing to learn something. I come out irascible and injured — you, enlightened. You're a keeper, Kasden. A gem. If you will have them, I will go on writing you letters, if only because a letter's lightness of step lets me walk in your shoes a little while.

When can I come see the shop?

—G

*Often Leed would draft letters in his notebooks. Other letters survive due to surveillance by the Market Optimization Bureau of his later correspondence, in particular with V. Kasden. Letters recovered (by secret means) from Bureau files will be noted in these pages.—Ed.*

\*

The Doctor has downstairs also a print of "The Art of Painting" by Vermeer. I remember seeing the original years ago, and on the little placard beside it a curator's inscription which took pains to note the 'theatricality' of the painting, emphasized supposedly by the curtain in the foreground 'held open with the thinnest of cords.' Even then this struck me as ridiculous. The very people entrusted to care for this work of art had hardly looked at it! It is from such seemingly inconsequential acts of carelessness — the failure to see — that injustice is sown. Later on, of course, it became useful to those in power to speak of 'theatricality' in art and thus degrade and marginalize it. But you need only look for yourself: the drapery is not tied back at all. No, it is being pulled aside! By whom? By the viewer, by you as you enter the painted studio. And look, an empty chair awaits you in the foreground. And so the painted artist and his model are depicted in the moment just before turning, just before recognizing the presence of the viewer in the room. And so you are each suspended — viewer, painted artist, and painted model — in the enclosure that precedes a work of art's opening to the natural world, to real life, non-fantasy, interruptions. The enclosure which precedes the breaking of the spell. Vermeer's picture is concerned with the inviolate artifice of painting (painting as both verb and noun). The picture celebrates and mourns this artifice. This is quite a different thing than base theatricality, for its dimensions of concern are different. Everything art shows us, it must show inside a frame. The moment the viewer looks, unadulterated reality is put to flight. Only the artist's process then, the action of creating the art in the absence of a viewer, can come anywhere near capturing a moment's truth, which is art's ideal. Here, having drawn back the curtain and stepped inside, we transgress the frame! We catch fleeting sight of the capture!

I have gone back downstairs in order to sketch in this notebook a copy of the painting.

*

Always, everything we see challenges us to understand. The extent to which we take up the challenge by our own wits and without resorting to prior interpretations is the extent to which we escape oppression.

*

I remember also, in the same museum as the Vermeer, the Brueghel painting from 1565, "Hunters in the Snow." How the artist so assuredly established the depth and perspective of his snowscape: its barren trees, its hunters in boots and animal skins, its receding slopes and distant houses and, in the middle distance, the wintery fields of white. The balance of all these elements is made to hang entirely upon a dark shape daubed at the practical center of the canvas. There, with perfect brazenness, the artist hung the black figure of a bird. The bird challenges the viewer to understand.

I'll draw it from memory now.

*The painting by Brueghel and the aforementioned work by Vermeer had, at the time of Leed's writing, been lost to public access or destroyed. Most copies were virtual iterations, many of these embellished or otherwise manipulated. Prints existed solely by samizdat. —Ed.*

*

Der Kunst ihre Freiheit. / For Art its Freedom.

*

Looked up from my desk to see — of all things — a peregrine falcon alight on the peak of the roof just below my window. I got up slowly and stood watching her. After a minute she fluttered into the nearby apricot tree, hiding amid the leaves, shaking the long black and white feathers of her tail. When I moved again she launched herself silently airborne over the fence, across the neighbor's yard, and out of view. Some moments, such abundance.

*

Sometimes, powerfully, one feels the loss of one's innocence toward language. And the effort to restore it always compromised simply by the need for such action.

*

Dare the reader to understand!

*

Visit to Kasden's must wait. Lethargy, headaches, disorientation, vertigo, high anxiety. But all these I've had before. An interruption, simply.

*

Two days later. No improvement yet.

Thought I'd just wait it out, but I begin to wonder if I should seek help.

Working very little and not at all, though my mind races.

*

I told myself, You live in a Doctor's house. So this morning, around the hour he customarily makes his breakfast, I loitered in the kitchen. It didn't take much for me to raise the subject once he'd laid eyes on me. Urgency outweighs embarrassment, times like this. He gave me a remote look, a little wariness in it, and asked politely one or two questions about my symptoms. I kept most of them in reserve, not wanting to alarm him, but suggested he might examine me a little. Well, there was no chance of that. He was shaking his head before I'd even got the words out — regretfully, granted. There's no coldness about him, but he's an extremely careful type and draws his lines where he will. With the recalled professionalism of the retiree he gave me a colleague's name and address.

So in the Doctor's very house one finds no medicine. *Doubtless Leed had not the money to visit another doctor.* —Ed.

*

I felt, as the Doctor looked at me across the kitchen counter, exactly like a boy of a certain age. The boy has not yet fully grown into his own face — you can see right into him through his eyes.

*

A little better today, 8 days since the onset. The world jolts, the vessel of the earth bumps sickeningly. Whomever knows to do so tightens their grip.

*

Passing the Whistler Nocturne again this evening while climbing the stairs with hot dinner dishes in hand, it suddenly occurred to me: what Impressionism captures is the culminating moment of the artist in exile. He is done with concessions and compromise. He will have his way or die (to quit his art would itself would be a death). From here forward he is an outcast in the modern world. Nothing can help him now but money or fame, and neither one can help his art. All later artists are his heirs in this. No regal court will have us anymore — we claim to need no court in any case. Where we used to make space in our work for the flattery of donors, now all is given over to our subject as we see it, as <u>we</u> want to treat it from canvas edge to canvas edge. Destiny is our patronage, even if it damns us. And we think, well, isn't everyone damned? — except that some in their time achieve higher expression than others.

Why, for all my gratitude to Impressionism, should I so resent it today? Artists opening a new way sometimes rupture things forever. And why shouldn't we desire some humane alternatives to alienation and marginalization?

Oh for a court now and then.

*

To Kasden's tomorrow.

*

Kasden's shop in the Northwest capital takes some finding, even for one in possession of the actual address, as I was. His clientele will find it by means even more challenging: a maze of associations, a connect-the-dots ordeal requiring the dialing of various telephone numbers, a secret trail of breadcrumbs. At last you come to the little apartment three floors above a red-awninged grocer's. These precautions, they're not because Kasden fears a raid (though he admits a raid is possible), but because any print outlet, being by nature un-Networked and non-Market-Optimized, is legally subject to punishing taxes and fees. Moreover, as I learned in the course of my visit, Bureau scrutiny is now a more or less permanent factor in his life. Offhand he mentioned that his M.V.R. has not just been demoted, as I'd assumed, but altogether revoked! He is defrocked, thus by law barred from further editing, let alone owning a shop. Though he is subject to careful monitoring, he does not believe he is being surveilled — yet. But precautions are important.

Anyway, I found the place at last. The apartment door was shabby and scarred. It rattled in its frame as I knocked. "Who is it?" called Kasden's voice from the other side. Then the opening door, his scruffy smile, a rough brotherly embrace, and he led me in among his wares. The space is very meager and not inviting. We stood on the stained, threadbare carpeting of the main room. There is no other room, only the narrow alcove of a kitchen, and in the opposite corner behind a rickety folding door, a toilet. There was the heavy discoloring smell of old kitchen grease, cooked cabbage, long ago meals, trapped steam.

He does not yet have many books. A single wide bookcase, about shoulder-high, is crammed with titles, and shored up beside this is a motley stack of others. At present this is his inventory entire. It is something though. More, certainly, than most people have got. And he's taken pains to ensure a rich selection. We stood there before the books, talking and talking as ever, pulling out volumes by turns, fanning the pages. And oh, once you begin to handle them, once their paper and covers rustle in your fingers, even that single modest bookcase begins to grow, all its dimensions opening up. And then something happens. From deep in the recesses of your sensual memory comes the recollection: the smell of a book-crowded space, of a bookstore or library. That was, you remember, the warm musty cream-colored smell of survival. The smell of a cared-for, touchable world. The smell of belief in spaces and rooms, in the idea that some things deserve keeping.

After a while Kasden put a kettle on and then we sat drinking tea. Or rather, I sat — there was only one chair — while Kasden leaned on the single windowsill. There is no bed or any other furniture to speak of. Kasden sleeps on a pallet that he rolls up by day — it was leaning in the corner. His aim is to use all the floorspace for shelves. He pictures a heady clutter of books, a tight labyrinth of cases, the walls lined floor to ceiling. There should be barely enough room to walk about, he says. And when I ask him where he will sleep he just shrugs and smiles. It's the least of his concerns. *The Doctrine of First Sale, which since 1908 had defended the prerogatives of a book's first owner, had been overturned long before. It was now of course illegal to lend, give, or resell books. This, given the scarcity of printed matter, was the most significant legislative means by which a mass shift to digital media was effectively made compulsory. —G.P.L.*

✳

Looking out his window onto the trash heaps in the street, the boarded windows, the shattered ones, the figures sprawling on the sidewalk and encamped before the vacant storefronts, Kasden says: "It began with the animosity toward print. That's where it started, you know. We gave up on the material world. We transferred all our faith to the promise of the disembodied marketplace. We wanted to believe in the perfectibility of data because flesh, you know, is so imperfect, corruptible. The aims seemed entirely noble at first, it was all in the interest of the long term — a living archive, universalized, undecayable. We thought we were conservators. We thought we were architects of our own culmination, a species at its apex. From this archive all knowledge, all progress, all prosperity. It was about opportunity, empowerment, equalization, accountability, checks and balances. What we never realized was how old, how deep-seated our impulses really were. How the whole enterprise could be traced back directly to the fear and loathing of the body, those ancient prejudices. We are doomed to yearn for the inorganic, whatever is clean and bright and painless. We've never quit hoping for heaven, its spaciousness and glow — even the nonbelievers among us. That deliverance from the encumbrance of our physical selves, from all the embarrassment and restriction of having a body. We believe we can strip away every unfortunate human attribute — our endless changeability, our mistake-making brains, our soiled and soiling hands, our damage-inducing habits, the pitiful limits of muscle capacity. We believe these things can be deleted, transcended in the glittering cosmos of the pixel, that we can quicken our own evolution, that we needn't be subject to nature and biology any longer but can master ourselves entirely —

the first self-programming species, outwitting even its own environment. And all this begins with an upload. In that instant whatever was self-contained, cumbersome, isolated in time and geography and subject to decay — that thing transcends its native limitations; now it is Networked, weightless, effortlessly searchable, essentialized, manipulable, eternal. If the thing is a book, that book is now considered redeemed. In its disembodiment, it is instantly universalized. Mass and weight are stripped away, the ink cannot be smudged, the paper can't be torn, in the backlit screen each page now carries its own light; the enclosure of the page itself — that restriction — is overthrown. What belonged to one now belongs to all. The book explodes outward, centripetal become centrifugal; mere text is gloriously transfigured into data, the absolution of bits and links, endlessly transmittable, evolvable, perfectible as information and commodity. One by one the book's individualized attributes are subject to deletion, purified by the Network; all the object's human properties — its spine, its edges, its mass, its mortality — removed. All this in the interest of human destiny, we are told. And yet—"

Here Kasden waves a hand over the demoralized scene outside the window.

"We never thought seriously about collateral. If all were virtualized, it was believed, there would be no collateral. That, we were told, was the beauty of those digital ideals from the start. That was the point: to do away with physical limitations. And because the

Network, early on, seemed so vital, so animate, so decentralized and thoroughly interactive — we believed it would all be possible! No wonder so many people turned away from print with such eagerness and speed, so happy to relinquish their books for Processing, so relieved to dump all that <u>weight</u>. It began there, didn't it, Geoff? All those people, that irresistible majority, they believed those tons of material could be universalized in that way. In fact, what they'd just done was to turn it over to the selective, limiting, sanitizing laws of a marketplace, a marketplace more eminently monitored and singly controlled than any in the history of the world. And a marketplace requires collateral, of course. A pixelated book, as it happens, constitutes an ideal form of collateral. So easily forgotten, untraceable, it never induces guilt or moral qualms about the system. Ostensibly eternalized, the disembodied book actually dies so much more easily than one of these."

He takes up in both hands a thick hardbound volume in marbled covers. An antique, its paper is gilt-edged, and the object itself seems to shimmer.

"Cumbersome, yellowing, the very imperfection of this thing from a hyper-technology standpoint, its temporality and limitation as a single object — <u>this</u> is the reason it has survived. Because it can be left lying just anywhere, or anyway that used to be the case. Because by nature it is eminently <u>discoverable</u>, whatever its M.V.R. might turn out to be. Because it cannot be monitored. Because it needn't conform to the mandates of Market Optimization or the keyword functionality of Network search. Stripping this book of its body, we strip away the natural laws of reading — serendipity, privacy, individualism, idiosyncrasy — in favor of what? Efficiency, commoditization, data integrity? And in <u>whose</u> interest exactly? The reader's? The writer's? No, the 'consumer's' — a very different creature. And now, of course, the chief interest served is that of the Bureau and its agents.

"An individual, now there's a creature that coheres and creates — the writer in words, the reader in mind. But the Network thrives on nothing so much as disassembly, <u>incoherence</u>. It appropriates or suppresses according to market demands. Its optimal operating condition is one of fragmentation and anomie. The collateral for collectivity is surveillance, loss of privacy, sabotage of individual expression. The collateral for virtualization…" Again Kasden gestures to the street below. "And the collateral for all our Futurity and despisal of the physical, material world? Loss of our humanity."

He returns the book to its case, shaking his head and smiling.

"You and me, Geoff, we resist this! We, in these shitholes of ours, we are the conservators now!"

*

<u>typographic</u>: adj. 1 produced by the art of printing 2 the style and appearance of printed matter.
<u>Electronic</u>: adj. 1a. Produced by or involving the flow of electrons b. of or relating to electrons or electronics 2 (of a device) using electronic components … electronic

publishing — the publication of books, etc., in a machine-readable form rather than on paper.

Technocracy: n. 1 the govt. or control of society or industry by technical experts 2 an instance or application of this.

Technopoly: n. 1 totalitarian technocracy 2 the systematic redefinition of history, art, truth, liberty, privacy, intelligence, communication, etc., to suit a new social order whose basis and aims are technological in nature 3 the use of technology for the total marginalization or imposed irrelevance of alternative or dissenting philosophies and production.

*

Definitions are important. Recalling them, we are spared the persuasions of convenient relativism. The dictionary not merely as fallback reference, but as forward beacon, as guide.

*

"And what's left when memory's gone — and your identity, Mrs. Smith?"
*Leed appears to be quoting a literary voice here. Reference lost.—Ed.*

*

conspiracy: n. 1 a secret plan to commit a crime or do harm, often for political ends; a plot.

custom: n. 1a. the usual way of behaving or acting b. a particular established way of behaving.

*

conformity: n. 1 action or behavior in accordance with

established practice; compliance 2 correspondence in
form or manner; likeness; agreement.

Society: n. 1 the sum of human conditions and activity
regarded as a whole functioning interdependently 2 a
social community 3a. a social mode of life b. the customs
and organization of an ordered community.

Coercion: n. 1 the act or process of persuading or
restraining (an unwilling person) by force 2
government by force.

*

Conspiracy theories consist of largely unverifiable
observations concerning fringe factors and elements;
i.e., phenomena not readily visible. Customs and culture
are another thing — they can be studied.

*

-Cave paintings at Chauvet: 32,000 years ago
-Earliest Chinese alphabets: 4,500 to 8,000 years ago
-Cuneiform: 5,000 BC – Mesopotamia (?)
-Hieroglyphs: 3,000 BC – Egypt
-Alphabet, Palestine: 1,700 BC (22 letters)
-Alphabet, Greece: 750 BC (24 letters)
-420 BC, Greece: orality begins to yield to literacy
-Codex: 55 AD – Rome: Caesar folds pages into
booklets for troop dispatches
-By 400 AD the codex has overtaken the scroll
-1455 AD: Typography developed and perfected into an
industry by Johannes Gutenberg

*

-Pictographic (cave art)
-Ideographic (hieroglyphs)

-Logographic > > > Phonographic (alphabets)

   ↓                 ↓

-Manuscriptic (scribal): tradition- and community-based

   ↓

-Typographic > > > Electronic: copyright- and intellectual-property-based

*

Socratic Greece, 5th-century BC: Alphabet/literacy already in existence, but oral culture remains preeminent. Information/knowledge is not yet widely portable — seeking it, you would go to an oral source. The digital device, far less durably portable than the book, has returned us to these pre-literate habits, a literally circumscribed intellectual life mandating that we plug in at a source (a screen). The terminal as the new Oracle. Being observed/surveilled in the Network today: analogous to being witnessed in the agora or Forum then. This historical regression implicit in the new technology...

*These entries represent the earliest evidence of Leed's formulations relating to what would become the Literary Resistance.—Ed.*

*

"The literate liberal is convinced that all real values are private, personal, individual ... Yet the new electronic technology pressures him towards the need for total human interdependence." —M. McLuhan

*McLuhan: reference unknown.—Ed.*

Still, always, even in the quiet of your room you face the onslaught. Endlessly you work to clear your vision against the day's overcrowding. You seek a single sheer coherent narrative of thought, the prolonged extension of a tone amid the broken broadcast noises, antic and ever-changing. You school yourself in history. You labor to remember: underlying the current complexity is woeful oversimplification.

Meanwhile you will know the truth by the serene simplicity of its surface. A shimmer, beneath which: depth, profundity, the unbroken quietude of the real.

*

Dream: I was an actor on a stage, in the midst of performing a beautifully tense and dramatic scene. The setting was a kitchen, the substance a cursory argument between me and another character — explosive emotions expressed with breathtaking restraint. Among my props was a melon knife and the performance required slicing a cantaloupe while I talked. I was halfway through the scene, deep in the pleasures of its progress, when by a slip of the knife I opened a spurting wound in my hand. Absolute, helpless terror at the sight of the blood! And yet without a thought I knew the scene would go on. I played the bleeding into the scene, going still deeper into the scene's thickly subdued emotions. The blood was running very fast, a puddle was pooling on the table where the open cantaloupe lay. I could see the horror in my fellow actor's face, but I gave no indication that I would permit us to break up the scene. The blood kept spilling and I went on, dragging my fellow actor with me, dragging even the audience, which by now was beginning to doubt the intentionality of the blood as it accumulated beyond the scene's proportions. As the scene drew on, its conclusion seemed to recede, the scene's emotions stretching off to new and longer intensity, and I began to wonder if I might lose consciousness right there on stage. But still I went on performing, performing and bleeding — for a powerful compulsion had overtaken me, the lit stage with its depths had me in thrall. I'd lost all control, the helplessness was delicious and rich. I couldn't be stopped.

*

And the dogs in nearby houses, howling descendent notes in empathy for the worrisome emergencies signified by distant sirens.

*

In relation to this book I think constantly of the Ecuadorian painting I once kept in my rooms: the chiaroscuro face of a man, one hand half-covering the face, one wide eye fixed on something inexpressible. The hand, the eye, the cheek bathed in a draining greenish light, all else submerged in the blackness of shadow.

I think also of the story of Lazarus, Book of John, chapter eleven. The stench of the tomb and the dead man in his wrappings coming from the darkness. I remember very well the depiction of this moment by

Giotto on his blue walls of the church in Padua. Lazarus upright before the mouth of darkness, his face still wound with cloth.

And I think of "The Partisan," the old song: "Oh the wind, the wind is blowing / Through the graves the wind is blowing / Freedom soon will come / Then we'll come from the shadows." As L. Cohen sang it, the song included the line: "These frontiers are my prison." Did he add this, I wonder?

*Giotto/church in Padua: While the church no longer stands, some virtual renderings of its paintings continue to be used in the digital tourism industry. / L. Cohen: reference unknown.—Ed.*

*

Magnetism decreases with distance from the poles. Ecuador, therefore, one of the 'lightest' places on earth?

What you want, amid the clomping and shaking, is an alembic Ecuador of the mind.

*

"Here I am a lord, at home a parasite." —Albrecht Dürer, on visiting Venice, 1505
*Albrecht Dürer: unknown personage.—Ed.*

*

*At the time of the following letter's composition, Leed had been writing fiction for 30 years and had completed four novels. Two of these,* Ragged Moon *and* Conundrums, *had gone to print some years before. Subsequently designated* Irrelevant *by the Market Optimization Bureau, both titles had been subjected to* Processing. *No known copies survive.*
*—Ed.*

Dear Kasden,

Tinkering tonight, unexpectedly and belatedly, on the manuscript of The Undreamt, I begin to see a little Providence at play in that book's fate. In other words, I think now that it could be — could be — for the best that the work has been suppressed so long, that for so long I have been compelled to live without the smallest prospect of its ever going to print. I'm growing as a writer. One never does stop, so long as one keeps working. My style, even — minor questions of which have seemed for a long time so consequential — is undergoing a change. I feel it in my attitude toward the sentence. It is an older writer, a more serious (if less earnest) one who reads over my finished work. This has always been true in a sense. It's the most common experience, a writer's urge to change what he's made. But it's happening on a more significant level with me now, I am more comprehensively altered in my outlook. And for the better, I feel. I see not only how to improve and strengthen a thing, but how I would do it differently from the outset. I do still have all the old convictions about The Undreamt, the rich experience I believe it waits to present to its reader, the useful and self-validating indignation about its prolonged obscurity, etc., etc. But I feel, too, a new confidence, a reassurance about the use, the value, of its painstaking progress toward the light of day. It will be, once it is finally printed, a stronger book even than I'd imagined, a thing more fully executed than at first envisioned. That is to say, the dividends of purgatory can be great.

It seems to me, anyway, worthwhile to think so.

All has been in order all the time. One must believe in one's work — in the process of change, of transformation, lying at the heart of the work. And one must have patience.

If our resistance to the age amounts to anything, Kas, if we manage by our bizarre and incremental labors to effect a revolution of any kind, maybe it will be just this: a revolution of <u>patience</u>.

That would be something, surely.

—G

The Undreamt *was my third novel, completed some five or six years earlier.*—G.P.L.

*

"It is sacrilege to pierce the mystic shell of color in search of form." —J.M.W. Turner
*Turner: an English Victorian painter.*—*Ed.*

*

The evensong of trees
The loyal dream of the sea
The Vedic dusk
The watertight flesh of the ripened orange

*

Last night, rather than installing myself at the desk, I lay in silence and shadows, one hand on these pages like a blessing.

*

"This is no book, / Who touches this, touches a man, / (Is it night? Are we here alone?) / It is I you hold, and who holds you, / I spring from the pages into your arms." —Whitman

*[Walter] Whitman: 19th-century American poet. His "Oh Captain My Captain" survives.—Ed.*

*

In the news is a family gone missing in the mountains a few hundred miles south of here. A search is underway. This family, traveling by car from their home in the Southern Territory, failed to check into their seashore hotel on the appointed day. Friends and relations raised the alarm after 24 hours. The family is believed to be stranded somewhere along the numerous snowy roads of the high passes in that mountain range. The Doctor follows their story avidly.

*

The small fears. Or rather the fear that fixes upon the smallest of things, all the little vials so easily broken, catastrophe dribbling out. The fear of infection, for example, never crossed my mind in earlier life. Now I find myself fretting to soak and daub every paper cut, every slightest bleeding scratch, with antiseptic wash.

More than merely aesthetic, more than finally spiritual, resistance must be bodily too.

*

The gathering of days, the passing years, and steadily the sense of peril increases. Person by person the ship loses passengers, and with the lightening of the vessel one feels all the more each swell, each plunge.

There is no captain and we are adrift. Clichés take on momentous gravity. The deeps drop away underneath,

*117*

the void yawns terribly overhead.

You find some comfort in the thought of maps — or try to. Maps are merely thoughts themselves. Figments and sketches. Approximations. Metaphors. And yet it is only metaphors, only the mind's pure reaches — lonely, loving, despairing — that can serve for ballast, really.

All things never quite water-tight.

In time the wind will tear away the sails.

The ship's very mast, deciduous.

*

Because we were the rarest of night creatures the darkness thrilled us to our loins. Because we counted rings of fallen trees we learned to reckon the hours.

*

Ich kann nicht ander.

*

Visit today from an Agent Keith. I heard voices in the stairwell, the Doctor bringing somebody up. To hear the Doctor projecting in that way, I knew at once he meant to alert me. The fact of a visitor in the house — this itself was reason to be on guard. The Doctor tapped at my door. "Uh, Mister Leed? Mister Leed, somebody here to see you." I'd gone to the closet, I was hurriedly dusting off the A/V device.

Now a knocking, a different fist, officious. Then a stranger's voice, instructing: "Mister Leed, open up please."

My device is a 12-inch, the smallest on the market. I'd lifted it to the bookcase and was restoring the volume — terribly obvious, I know, the sudden blaring of audio. The visual was multiple male heads talking, each disembodied in its own little box. One was angry and spewing, one just laughed, a third was groomed and stern. But now I was crossing to the door, where the man was positively thumping. I opened it and there was the Doctor, uncharacteristically hunched, a bit cowed alongside our imperious caller. He'd aged himself, I saw. It would win him some leniency — and justify his slowness leading the visitor upstairs. He gave me an old man's blank look. "An Agent Keith for you, Mister Leed."

The agent was coiffed in their up-to-the-minute, self-satisfied way. A shading of stubble just enough to scratch. A cardigan, sleeves pushed to the elbows. A black tie, loosely knotted, unironed shirt collar like a cowlick. He had a name badge on one lapel. He wore a pair of Network-enabled glasses and carried his digital clipboard under one arm. He stepped right in, eyes on my A/V device, and murmured over his shoulder, "Thank you, Doctor."

The Doctor shrank away down the stairs.

"Hi, Mister Leed. Mind if I call you Geoffrey?"

"Sure. No Problem."

"Great. I'm here today for your Courtesy Audit, Geoffrey." His glazed eyes weren't even seeing me, he was busily processing the data his lenses displayed for him. He flipped the clipboard onto his forearm and his fingers fidgeted on the glass. "Our quota records show your transmission stream pretty normal the last couple of months, Geoffrey."

"Okay."

"However, prior to that there was a period of, let's see, several <u>weeks</u> that's all but black. Was this old beast knocking you offline?" He placed a knowing hand on the console.

"Actually it was in storage. I was on the move, not really settled in any one place, so there wasn't much opportunity."

"I see. And you have no mobile device, correct, Geoffrey?"

I knew I was on record. "Correct."

"So mobile log-ons are out of the question," he pronounced. A verdict, clearly.

He was turning about, taking in the room, and I noticed a small gray earpiece. In that moment his finger came up to graze it as if idly scratching. He seemed to nod and when he turned back to me he said, "Your occupation, Geoffrey, is it still Writer?"

"Yes."

"And your writing methods, if you don't mind me asking, Geoffrey."

What a question. How to boil down a life, a lifetime's work? But I knew what he was asking. I shrugged. "Analog."

He knew this well enough. It was all there inside his slim oracle of glass, plastic, and silicon — or rather, inside the gurgling bits of some master memory somewhere offsite, "offshore" in fact. Or "in the cloud," as they preferred to say (deliberate intimations of godliness, omniscience). Right at that moment the cloud lords were reviewing my data stream. Keith and the Bureau know very well what I am <u>not</u> doing. It's whatever I am doing that they <u>cannot</u> know that obsesses them, harmless as I may be. Their appetite for data is insatiable. Alarms sound wherever the data is short in supply — dearth of data indicates non-compliance.

Keith was frowning. He was assuming a philanthropic air of concern. "Somebody as creative as yourself, Geoffrey, you understand the range of opportunity available to you. The promotional capacity, the professional networking bandwidth, not to mention the <u>efficiency</u>. To be very frank, Geoffrey, we at the Bureau don't like to see people like you — people of your <u>potential</u> — getting, well, let's face it, getting left behind."

He paused, seeming to await my response. Really he was scanning his lenses again, receiving further instruction via earpiece.

"For a Content Generator like yourself," he went on, "it's never been easier to Market Optimize. Your audience is out there — everyone has one — and it's just waiting to tell you what it wants! You understand, Geoffrey, that the Network is all inclusive, it has no overruling identity, it's completely User Defined. That's its beauty. You could think of it, if you want, as one big Dream Actualization Machine. All it takes is getting on board."

What could I say to this? Having no idea, I thought it best to simply nod.

"Getting on board is what people do, Geoffrey. They do it because, well, being left behind is just no fun. You get on board because it's in your own best interest."

Keith went on a while before tapping a transmission into his clipboard. The wonders of Wireless in that instant deposited a series of coupon codes into the credit column of my Digital Profile. These entitled me to any of numerous mobile devices at special discount. It was pure formality. Neither of us mentioned the innumerable identical coupons already stored in that column.

Salesmanship dispatched, Agent Keith's manner turned crisp. "Now to the subject of V. Kasden."

"Sorry," I said. "Who?"

We went through the motions from there, each man faithfully playing his role. It was a cool and mechanical exchange, the System manifesting all its coercive protocol in the quiet confines of my harmless little room. We reviewed my Market Viability Rating, we "got on the same page" about healthy Optimization efforts versus Audits and prospective censures, and Keith said, "You do understand that Mister Kasden's M.V.R. has been revoked."

Once or twice more I saw the agent pretend to scratch his ear — the slight roll-back of his eyes as the tiny speaker buzzed instruction into his brain. The faces on my A/V device grinned, mooned, guffawed.

As he was leaving, before he'd even shut the door, I'd killed the volume and was moving the device back to the closet.

*

What were you? What are you now? You've told
yourself a story all this time, and the story has misled
you — that there can be two wars, more. No. There is
only one war. You and your comrades will fight it the
only permissible way. ... You might have been in a
position like mine by now, there's no reason why not.
This, however, is no longer possible. Of course you
know this. A man is given his chance. He takes it or he
doesn't. He fights for something or for nothing. But let
me ask you, and I mean this quite seriously, I want to
know: What did you think you stood to gain?

*

The Doctor came through the visit fine. I felt it my
duty to check on him. At his age he's exempt from most
Transmission Quotas. The Bureau has, in recent years,
upped the intake margin for folks of his generation, but
there's little to be done to enforce it, given that the
M.V.R. is of scant importance for most everyone in his
stage of life.

"I never understand how they find people," the
Doctor told me. "I didn't register you."

"It wasn't you," I assured him, "it was my
transmission stream." And I explained how I try to let
them see it, so they can't claim I'm hiding.

He seemed dismayed by this. Clearly he doesn't like
the prospect of further visits. I did my best to assure
him I would vacate if pressure appeared to be
mounting. This relieved him some. He stared at the
floor a minute, then with a small wave of his hand

beckoned me to follow him. We walked the downstairs hallway to its end and stood just outside his bedroom door.

"Since things keep getting worse," he said, "I think you ought to see this."

He stooped and turned back the frayed edge of the green hallway runner, then knelt and began working his fingers along a seam in the flooring. After a moment he'd pried up a rectangular section of boards. A musty scent of underflooring arose. He moved a plank of loose plywood aside and there between the exposed joists, laid neatly in and dully shining, was a stack of silver bullion.

So the compact is sealed between us. We trust each other, the Doctor and me.

✳

Agent Keith left me a pamphlet — an actual printed artifact, which goes to show the avidity of their 'outreach.' While the content is all too well known to anybody in these times, I transcribe, for the benefit of those who may come after us, a few choice excerpts. First, a bit of M.O.B. self-definition:

"The Market Optimization Bureau was founded upon these universally acknowledged principles: a) the Network is a monumental advance in human communications, propelling modern society toward previously unimagined levels of freedom, empowerment, and material security b) success is the primary desire of all people c) all people wish to be optimally connected to their friends, family, and customers, and d) this optimization is best achieved through technologically enabled, helpful, and efficient governance. The Market Optimization Bureau is dedicated to the mission of Network Preeminence, of ensuring that all people belong to the Network, and that the Network serve all people's desire for optimized marketing and communications. Our Agent Outreach Program, a division of the Bureau's Program for Economic and Objective Purity in Literary Enterprise, is perhaps the most important component of our ongoing work to achieve Universal Optimization."

The pamphlet I was given is one of many textual variations, each thematically targeted. Thus the back page of mine includes "Guidelines for Success in Writing Fiction." A few samples: Item #2—"Do not alienate or estrange readers by giving them words, worlds, or characters they may have difficulty recognizing." Item #4—"Give every story a beginning, middle, and end." Item #8— "Do not rely on metaphor, allegory, satire, or literary or historical references in writing your story. It should be a story strong enough 'to stand on its own two feet.'" Item #11—"Remember, you don't need to — and shouldn't — write alone. Take advantage of the Market Optimization Bureau Composition Collective to get your story written AND market-optimized all at once!" Item #14—"Use the Network every day to establish and maintain your readership base. If you do not know what readers want, ask them! Remember, an unread writer is not in fact a writer."

\*

The stranded family: the Doctor informs me their vehicle was found today, mired in snow along an old abandoned forestry road. Inside, the wife and two children were alive, though cold and hungry. The husband set off in search of help two days ago and is still missing. Before going, he removed the vehicle tires so the wife could burn them for heat. She's been breastfeeding her children, an infant and a five-year-old, throughout their 72-hour ordeal. The disaster began with the family's global tracking device. The mountains were to be the shortest route to the sea, or so said the digital display, colorful with confidence. People everywhere are following the story now, chilled by every detail. A helicopter has carried mother and children out of the mountains.

But where is the father? Mysteriously, his shirt has been found in a ravine.

\*

A note from Kasden: "Has our friendly Bureau come to see you lately?"

# 3.

# In Country

# JOSEPHA

*I would ask him, What side are you on? Many, many times I would ask him this. And I came to believe he was just avoiding the question. I understood only later: he truly never knew how to answer.*

*I would ask him, Is that really your name? Janos? And of course I knew it was not his name. Still, he was never anything but Janos to me.*

*Forever now, he said, you will have to live with those horrible things blocking out the sky. You and all the people in this sector.*

*On my window the rain was tapping, blurring the world. We lay in bed together, watching the evening's pink glow beyond the concrete towers the Army had put up the month before. Anti-aircraft towers, two stood in view from my window, their tops manned with great guns. They were erected in a period of three weeks, smack in the center of the nearby park, and they were massive, stupendous. Each one, I'd been told, could house 30,000 troops.*

*Even after the war, said Janos, they'll still be there. They'll be as horrendously ugly as ever, and all the people who lived through this time — all those people who wish only to forget — those people will have to bear the sight of them everyday.*

*They'll be victory monuments, I said. Indestructible tributes to the indestructible Army.*

*No, said Janos, not even moving. They will only be part of your punishment.*

*But look at them, so big and hard, I said, and I reached down for him. Doesn't that stir you?*

*No. It is only your touch that stirs me, he said.*

*And he rolled so I could have him between my thighs.*

*Janos. Nameless boy. Never was another man as wholly naked for me as you were. Never, after the knife and blood, could I be as naked for anyone.*

*There are no sides.*

*I repeat this now, as I touch myself.*

*There are no sides.*

*Today again the rain is streaming down my window. The towers are out there, dark and horrible. No one will ever tear them down. And yet, through the water on the glass, they waver.*

. . .

In darkness, approaching, what he'd believed to be the stone face of a cliff revealed itself a church.

Jude stood a minute wondering. Was this a further vision? Was it the syringe that saw church where only craggy stone could be? But he walked up to it and touched its wholly material door and awoke to soberness.

He pushed and the door creaked heavily. In the total blackness within, the door, as it swung, seemed to submerge.

He stepped over the thick stone threshold, half-expecting to sink on the other side. His heel came down with a birdlike flurry of whispers on solid floor. The noise sped upward to invisible heights, an ancient faraway rustling of the blackness. He'd announced himself.

But how vast was this place? How tall? Sufficient to house a regiment at least. It had the empty, open feeling of the plains he'd just crossed. Its dark felt darker than the night outside.

He pushed shut the great door. In blindness he slumped down beside the wall and sleep slumped atop him like a second body.

Then he was in a well and sinking and the dark was ever darker.

Till he seemed to touch bottom where there was, he

realized, another door, and somebody pushing it open
from the other side, and light was fanning along its
edges like wings—


He awoke on stone floor. He seemed to be in a tunnel of
kinds. Far at the other end a light was bobbing toward
him. The dark head of whomever carried the light. The
dark legs of whomever, traveling in spokes of gold.

Then Jude was blinded and could only wave his
hands.

Are you alone? said a voice.

The lamp swung to see for itself.

Are you hungry?

# SEXTON

*Wartime or not the doors of a church ought never to be locked*
*— not unless there be hordes of infidels rampaging with*
*torches at the portals or bent upon destruction some other*
*way. Now I do not encourage foolishness nor claim it our*
*righteous duty to welcome any kind of hate. But look here, for*
*nine centuries the church has stood on this spot. It is by any*
*reasonable view a mountain amid mountains. I mean it's*
*now a thing of nature, all but geological. Stand in the*
*transept and feel the spiritual crosswinds. The man-labor*
*that vaulted this church is no less a force of God than the*
*rivers and winds that carve caves in the wild, or the earth's*
*stirrings which lift those peaks and crags clothed half the year*
*in ice.*

*Yes, church this old is God's wonder. And that it's seen*
*some comings and goings you can be certain. It does not*
*shudder at this war. Has it borne hard treatment in its time?*
*Has it borne abuse? To be sure. Religious zealots plastered*
*the old frescoes over. Political fervor smashed the altars and*
*disinterred bodies from the crypt. Worse. Go and read the*
*record books.*

*Oh but though the world turns and swirls the church stays*
*still and doors stand open. It's no single person's place, no*
*nation's, no village's. It belongs to everyone.*

*Twenty-six years I've made my bed in the chancel behind a screen. The chancel itself has a screen of course. My chamber thus doubly screened, the drafts stay out and I keep comfortable as a cottager. I've got a pallet of goosefeather, a spirit lamp, and a peatstove that keeps off the chilblains in winter. Standing at the foot of my bed it lets me hook my heels at the fender as it were all my dreaming hours.*

*With the church mice and church rats I have an understanding — they don't keep me up.*

*Likewise the ghosts and other persistencies which number as plenty.*

*Likewise the voices. A vault this old and vast you see will house forever each choir song each whispered prayer each chanted matins and vespers, much the way the vaulted heavens house the streaming light of a star long after some galactic wind came to snuff it.*

*Or have you ever slept out a summer night in the deep forest to hear in the stillest waking hour the harmonic memory of the trees? They hum a very high quiet fluty kind of note — the note of the wind or their memory of it. Well an ancient church is no different. Kind of a living memory a church like this is. Which gives you the sense upon crossing the threshold inside that the church stands separate and you're now in a different world.*

*It's the same world of course, only a part you don't often visit. Usually you forget it's there at all. Never do you really get to know and understand it. No, even to the sexton of twenty-six years waking and sleeping inside it this corner of the world is mystery. It will remain so I reckon till my turn comes to take up residence in that echoing chorus. You can never understand, never arrive there till then. For now, you get hints and sensations. For our purposes those are enough anyway. I believe not much more is expected of each of us in his time save to heed the hints a little. I've never properly laid eyes on a spirit, for example, though one night for a great long while I could've sworn I was doing just that — indeed, talking with one at length.*

*He was only a man though after all. I know it because he stayed some time.*

*But having taken him for a spirit at first, something of that world-within-world, something like a scent, clung to him all the time after. Clung to us both I suppose.*

*We lived a greater memory me and that fellow.*

. . .

There were vestments and priestly stoles hung about the chancel, but the little man, cassocked though he was in a baggy thing of jute or coarse wool, said he was neither priest nor monk. Caretaker only. He did, he confessed, wear the robes for warmth in colder months.

From his modest store he gave Jude a miraculous square of cheese, only slightly blue along one edge. Also a morsel of meat, unidentifiable. Jude didn't ask what it was.

The sexton poured him water in a wooden cup. He watched Jude eat and drink.

Are you in danger? he asked at last.

Jude said, No one's following me, if that's your meaning.

Soldier?

No.

Deserter?

No.

The sexton sat back on his crude little stool. Hands folded atop his knees, he seemed content to quit his questioning. Jude thanked him for the food and water.

In the morning you can take a bath, said the sexton. And I hope you will stay as long as you wish. This is my home and you are welcome here.

. . .

Next morning Jude woke on the chancel floor to the soft noises of the sexton astir at the stove.

The church was only less dark, not light. He realized all the windows were boarded. Sun leaked in through gaps and joints.

The sexton's lamp was alight at the man's side. A kettle plumed steam. He was stirring a pot.

Jude had thought he heard footsteps, or a knocking at one of the distant doors. Now, lying on his back atop the oddments of garment the sexton had put down for bedding, he saw small shapes aflicker in the dimness and understood that birds were flapping in the pyramidal heights above.

The sexton had turned his head. Stew's my regular breakfast. You should share this.

The odor was pungent, wholesome. The very kind of meal for a church.

Jude rolled to his side and heaved himself up, grunting, to sit. What happened to the windows? Blown out?

The sexton's head shook. His hair was a dying brown all clotted with gray. Took them out. He ladled a serving into a bowl and passed it. In the half-dark the steam shot very high. They're all handworked panels. Thirteenth-century. Hundreds of pieces in each. They had to come down part by part. Took more than a year, but that was better than seeing them blasted out once the war reached us.

The bowl was scorching Jude's hands. He nested it into his bedding. The same indeterminate mincemeat skiffed amid wilted greens, tatters of carrot, and nubbins of potato or yam.

You had help? said Jude, considering those heights again. Clerestory of wood and birdshit now.

Some at first. Once the Army got close the others fled. Would've been fools to stay, God knows. I finished the job myself.

And that wasn't foolish? For you to stay?

The sexton merely smiled over the bowl in his hands. He'd sunk to his little cobbler's seat again. Twenty years I'd looked after this church. That's like a marriage. One hand moved back and forth before him. And the church doesn't run. A little war couldn't divorce us.

Jude hunched over his bowl. Fed himself in silence.

I'm sorry, said the sexton. I see it's been no little war for you. And you've gone a long time without a proper meal, yes?

Jude shrugged. He didn't care to claim much suffering.

The other Army, of course, had come and made quarters in the church. Those first several days the sexton had hid himself high in the dark triforium. But they meant to stay awhile — and when they began firing pistols into the ceiling to drop the birds, he made himself known to them.

Why hide from us, sexton? they'd said. We never wanted to harm you, we're men of the same faith — and after all there's no hiding from this Army, it sees everything.

He was permitted to live among them, though he must sleep on the floor, the Lieutenant-Colonel having appropriated the chancel with its bed and stove.

They asked him many times, Why the boarded windows?

Given answer, they smiled sardonically. We wouldn't have hurt them, why would we hurt your windows?

He saw they lacked sense for the beautiful fragility of old glass.

They stayed a fortnight. The soldiers lounged and smoked.

They built campfires in the aisles, warmed themselves and cooked and slept as if under the stars.

They were caked in filth from the battlefields. Many had dead, staring, crustaceous eyes.

The officers, though, were lively and crisp. Upon the old altar they unrolled great maps and conferred like architects. They believed they were building a world.

They made a hospital of the south chapel. Their dead were stacked along the walls for days at a time, white in blankets of quicklime.

The sexton they left alone, mostly. Now and then he would carry their water, to keep in their graces. They pretended, at least, to respect him, his office here.

Finally they left. The south chapel, emptied behind them, was ankle deep in lime. The bleached whiteness rose mold-like along the stone walls to the height of a man.

Jude stayed on in the church.

The queer mincemeat of the sexton's stew, he learned, was bird and mouse. The man hunted these with sprung traps and sometimes a sling. In the church's high stone crannies he was agile as a spider. Amid the coiled stairwells and laddered fretwork of the old towers he'd constructed roosting places where he would sit or recline, sometimes for most of a day, awaiting the clatter of a nearby trap.

By daylight, too, he would walk the slanted aluminum roof, up under the broken arcades of the buttresses where the wind whistled and jagged pebbles skittered underfoot.

And he still rang the bell everyday at noon. This task he regarded as religious duty. Drawing a line from heaven to earth, he called it. That's the church's business, or who will do it? he said.

Jude, climbing behind him to the bell tower at his bidding, watched the sexton haul on the rope with all his weight, feet swinging up off the platform. He did seem to be tugging a single great thread earthward from the sun.

The iron tongue hammered in the dark cauldron above them. They'd plugged their ears with tallow, but their bones clanged and Jude's hair bristled and the platform shook. In the world he was coming from, he'd forgotten the authority of such a bell.

There had once been a village in the shadow of the church, but it had vanished long before. Centuries, reckoned the sexton. With the first peat mining in the region, the houses were all taken apart and moved nearer the bogs some miles off. For generations the miners and their families had retraced the way to the church several times a week, but the war stopped them coming, and for years now the church had lacked a priest. Still, the sexton stayed and rang the bell whose sound carried over the country, and once, sometimes twice a month, the ladies of the village would bring the sexton cheese or bread, whatever could be spared, each gift gotten up by collection among the villagers. Their houses now clustered around industry, they no longer came to worship or pray, but they did not forget their shuttered church, regarding it, still, as heart and center of their lives.

We are, all of us, always seeking what a church like this can offer, said the sexton. Isn't that what brought you here?

It was late and they were settling in for the night. There was an awful draft blowing along the chancel floor.

Jude, on his back under his coverings, had started to shiver. He said, Me, I came by chance. I was walking and found this place in my path.

Oh, but sometimes we seek and know it not.

Though he believed nothing of the kind, Jude did not dispute this. He was not meant for saving. The long war, itself his own recurring death, had leveled every wall. All borders had bled away and every threshold seemed a figment. There was no place anymore to hang that door called Salvation, let alone walk through it. And there was no need. Every room he entered was himself. This was no blessed state, no beatitude. The oneness of all things was an unexpected loneliness.

There's no sense you shivering on the floor, said the sexton, pulling back his blanket. My bed is narrow, but warm is better than wide.

For a time Jude remained on the floor. Then he climbed up and dragged his coverings after.


One day they stood together in the musty crypt. Jude held a torch as the sexton opened a crate. Inside were stacks of glittering glass panels couched in excelsior. There was the resinous smell of pine as the sexton brushed the shavings away.

Hold the torch behind it, he said, lifting out a square of glass large as a dinner plate.

Together they saw, looking back at them from the flickering colors, two small faces. Some kind of workmen in tunics, with angular brows and dot eyes. The workmen were bent to a task. Each held an antique hammer.

Church builders, said the sexton. Stone masons.

They were hammering at chisels. The lower panel,

detached now, would have shown the stone they worked. Against a blue horizon just above their heads hung a set of crimson calipers.

Jude, dazed, saw again the black crypt before his torch as the panel sank in the sexton's hands.

Here, another. The sexton raised a rectangle showing a headlong white dove. Behind the fan of wings were the gables of a royal house in golds and greens. Holy Spirit, he explained.

You know all the meanings? said Jude.

But the sexton didn't hear. Panels clinked in the shaky light.

They stared at another: a man was pulling a sword from a yellow scabbard, his face vacant, his mouth grimly horizontal, his eyes on the back of an unsuspecting traveler. Behind the figures trees sprouted in many colors.

Tale of the Good Samaritan, said the sexton.

They stood in that dark a long time more, regarding other ancient faces, ancient colors. Kings and knights and commoners. Enhaloed saints and Christs and pronghorned Satans. Beasts, birds, flowers, fortresses, angels.

Garnished, murmured the sexton, with all manner of precious stones, jasper, sapphire, chalcedony, emerald, topaz, jacinth, amethyst. It seemed something he'd memorized. That's Heavenly Jerusalem, he said.

In the torchlight the brilliant forms seemed to jerk and caper.

Then the sexton said, What is it you search for?

I told you, said Jude. Nothing.

The sexton, still holding a windowpiece, had turned his head to look at him, his face a quilt of color. He that loseth his life, he said, shall save it.

Jude stood the man's study and made no reply.

He felt that he had no life to lose. He was no proper self and therefore no proper death, symbolical or actual, could await. He'd let slip somewhere, or had had torn from him, the I of identity. He was a blowing dust that got in under doors, a wind, a shadow, a smell. And if he was a shadow it was of no single shape but a mass of shapes, a murk, like the shadow of a forest at the edge of a field.

For him to hear the words *He that loseth his life shall save it* was to see the men and women heaped in a ditch, the staved scalps and the blood all gummed.

Those deaths were his, he had become them. He was both man and woman brained and bled in mud. He was also their killer — the Enemy or Ally who had done it. Whatever pity that was due was due to him, whatever blame due to him. Whatever man he used to be had been taken by both hands of this war and shaken, shaken like a cloth down to threadwork, a loose mesh that could hold nothing, obscure nothing, protect nothing.

He was of no consequence.

He was no single person but — somehow, painfully — everyone.

*He that loseth his life shall save it.*

Had *they* been saved, then, those tangled dead too plentiful to count?

At night, as the season brought its first midnight frosts, the sexton began to clutch under the blankets, breath sultry on Jude's neck. Jude lay, submissive, as the hands searched and inquired. Even this devoted little man, steward of the personal salvation, would seep half-wakeful over the lip of identity.

The church would creak in the night like an old ship.

Drafts whirred in the nave and birds groaned overhead and mice skittered across the chancel floor.

The sexton would murmur at Jude's neck. He'd heard the voices of ghosts, he said, could hear them now. Could Jude?

Listen!

The sexton said that in the time since the Army had gone a woman in the village had pronounced him a spy, claiming he'd struck a pernicious bargain while living those weeks amid the Enemy. He said he'd lately noticed the women, while bringing him food each week, behaving toward him with newly sidelong eyes.

He told how he'd never known a family and had come here twenty-six years ago a runaway from warden parents in the south.

He asked did Jude ever have a family, but received no answer.

The sexton said sometimes he could hardly believe he'd ever had another life, that he hadn't been born in this very chancel, that he held claim to only this one contemporary world. To live so long in a church was to lose track of time altogether, to confuse the ancient and changeless with now. Ever since the windows had been boarded this confusion even came to bear upon night and day, so that sometimes, climbing out onto the roof, the daylight struck him like a lightning bolt.

He told how the church, three or four centuries ago, had started to lean at the outside walls owing to some error in the original design, and how a massive iron chain had been fastened about the upper walls to brace it, and how this chain remained there even still and was all that kept the towers of stone from cascading down, and how in the zenith of certain seasons the chain would expand or contract so that there came a great nautical cracking in the heights.

He told a memory he had from a book, of Magellan and his crew adrift and starving in a tropical sea, and how they'd been forced of necessity to eat the leather stripping from the yards of the ship. ...

Then his breath softened on the back of Jude's neck, his hands relaxed in the blankets, and snuffling sleep would overtake him.

·  ,  ·

Jude would wake hours later to the tickling drum of tiny feet about the pillow and coverings. Hungry mice scavenging for crumbs.

The suspicious woman had had a daughter, the sexton explained in days after. The soldiers during the occupation had raped and killed the girl.

Sabina, she was called. There was such outrage in the village. Soon enough the soldiers learned that the people were rallying for attack. They'd burn the church down over the brutes if they must — their fury was that great. That was finally why the Army left. The Major-General wanted nothing to do with the vengeance of those families.

I think of her often now, of little Sabina. How her death was a toll to make the soldiers go.

Yes, said Jude. Always there's a toll.

He wrote his name just here, said the sexton. Do you see?

They stood together in one of the porticoes with the statuary of saints and prophets shoulder to shoulder in rank above them. Jeremiah held a shield, a headless man his head. Abraham cupped his child's cheek against his loins, the boy's feet bound between his own, and readied a stone to smite him.

*Adumbrareus*, do you see? *Adumbrareous made this.* The church builder.

Jude looked at the words etched with remarkable clarity across the stone lintel. Above the words: the chiseled robes of the savior in his tympanum, arms outstretched in majesty.

Seven centuries ago he put his name here. No other church of his time bears a name. He was making a point, you see? Names are important, even if you are not a saint, a king, a prophet.

The sexton was making a point of his own. He, too, knew that Jude's name was not Jude.

They call it the Cult of Carts, the age that built all these churches, because the workers, the architects, are all anonymous. The finished church, its glory, was all that mattered. You see, there was no *personal* salvation then. But Adumbrareus, carving his name here, says, 'God knows me!'

149

The sexton squeezed Jude's shoulder. He'd grown very insistent. Call our age the Cult of Guns. No matter. God knows each of us, my friend. God knows *you.*

His eyes glistened and seemed to well. I am Simeon, he said.

Jude, seeing that the sexton awaited answer, said, And you know my name.


Again in the night, under blankets, the sexton talked.

He'd had a twin, he explained. He'd known his twin inside the womb only, for the child was stillborn. Their mother, in grief, saw her surviving boy — how lusty-lunged and wiry he was — and refused to suckle him. In the deep of her womb this creature had somehow learned treachery. It would mark him now, Child of Cain. Before he could ever be hers, she disowned him. *Don't show me his face! Take him!*

She was insane, or so said his warden parents, who told him the story once he'd come of age. According to village rumor, she'd raved of having suffered the twins wrangling in her belly — she'd long felt one of them gaining the upper hand, working, always working, to siphon off the other's strength. His mother died, he was told, within a year of his birth — a madwoman on the streets.

I've often thought, said the sexton, that the child I outlived was a brother. Nobody ever told me but I knew. Is it memory? I cannot call him to mind, but I *did* see him once — the first thing I ever saw. Can we remember such things?

The sexton's embrace grew stronger.

God brought you here. You see? It was no accident. God's business is brotherhood, and we are brothers, you and I.

Jude lay silent. At the foot of the bed the peat stove was ticking.

*X had said, I know what you will do, my brother, and I'm not afraid.*

Again warm breath washed over Jude's neck.

Why should you hide yourself? We know each other from long ago. Tell me where you've come from. Why do you hide? Tell me your name.

Jude, feeling now the smallness of the vast church, didn't answer.

He was asked again and again he didn't answer.

Then the sexton began pulling at the mice-nibbled blankets. The bed began to shudder, and Jude heard the muffled noises of the sexton crying. The sexton began to push: Go! Go!

He'd left Jude the tattered top blanket. This Jude trailed from his shoulders as he crept from the chancel in the dark.

Out in the hollow church, all stone and frigid night, the blackness was nothing like a womb.

Jude awoke curled upon guano-caked floor in the cracked daylight of the nave.

Birds were clapping high above. Little dollops of shit were falling. After them, more slowly, came bits of spiraling fluff and straw. A nest in the making — or the raiding of one.

He raised his head. Seeing the floorstones patterned around him in a spiral, he saw he'd slept upon the ancient labyrinth.

There came a scraping noise and Jude turned to find the sexton in sackcloth, on his knees. His face a ruin of tears, he was knee-walking along the labyrinth, moaning penitence. He seemed blind to Jude's presence.

Leaving the thin blanket behind him on the floor, Jude gathered his pilgrim bag and walked to the church door. The sexton said nothing, only keened to the vacant nave.

The day was bright and windy, all burning gold.

Again Jude was starting out — and to be going was no special burden. He'd never meant to stay.


He walked in hunger all the morning. By noon he was in a rocky ravine, tracing the course of a dry creek bed vaguely east. Still the wind was blowing in the scrub-brush. Every now and then it carried up a fine sheet of sand and gristle that prickled like nettle at his ears, his neck, the backs of his wrists.

Though he'd gone some distance, a breath of a sound came after him all the way and halted him in the sun. He stood and turned toward it.

High off and almost secretive, a bell was clanging in the tower of a church.

From the oldest of the old stories Jude knew the conceit. Of character revealed and defined by virtue of destination, objective, a fixed goal.

A man walking walked always toward something. A man fighting fought with cause, mind and heart bent upon a prize. The quest was all, a matter of time and endurance. For the sake of the quest a man's will could weather any hardship and transcend any wound. The spirit was a bowsprit fixed upon a mark, the body the keel that cleaved the waters. The vessel may come to harbor, it may not, but the harbor was its ultimate dream.

So it was said.

For Jude, though, something darkly shimmering guided him, and it was *everywhere*, and in secret it caused all things to seep together, and it belied the stringent solidity of maps — leading him to no single destination.

The shimmer, because it was always in everything, was always deniable. You walked and felt its wavering underfoot. You thought you saw a scintillation, a gesture as of water. But turning your head to spot it, all things cooled and crackled solid again. It was not to be recorded.

And yet it was there in the way the bodies had floated in the pond, even there. In the glassy vacuities of open eyes that no longer stared. In the dark circles of open mouths.

The surface of the swamp had reflected sky.

Did the bodies float in water or upon the air?


A man walking walked always *through* something. *From, past, toward* — these were of less importance. The dead did not vanish from the earth. Out of sight merely, they were among you, just here, just there.


*Josepha...*


One day in the capital, soon after the Enemy occupation was overthrown, Jude had been in Topa Precinct, disguised in Army uniform. Passing along a busy sidewalk, he noticed two soldiers at work in a doorway across the street. From a metal hand truck between them they were unloading something. Part of the cargo flopped to the pavement as they struggled to transfer the rest. They intended to deposit it there against the wall.

The flopping parts were hands and legs, belonging to a man so limp and bloodied he might have been mistaken for a heap of soiled towels.

The soldiers managed to unfold him onto the sidewalk, then with a few slow kicks pushed his legs into the shadow of the wall, out of the pedestrian traffic.

Finished, they trundled their cart back inside and shut the door.

In broad daylight the body lay waiting. For what?

# DEAD MAN

*They thought I was a Partisan. I was never much of anything, but some rumor reached them or I bore a certain likeness.*

*Mistakes like this are common. Anyway, the dead are not interested in blame. In books, old stories, plays, the ghosts want vengeance. No. Vengeance is for the living. It was for them — the ones who arrested, detained, interrogated, and tortured me. They had the idea that they could put something right. It was not a surprise. My family had seen much of the Army in the recent days.*

*Until then, though, I knew nothing of their methods, their resourcefulness. Of these, most people are unaware. What can you know of such rooms, the tables and straps? I was a baker.*

*But you come to see — it takes only a few moments — the levels of ingenuity, attention to detail, that mankind has developed. No single generation is to blame for these systems. They come of devoted study, through the ages.*

*There were lights in my eyes. Lights, lights, until all that could come of this was blackness. What they wanted were words and names, and in reaching for these they strangled, choked, suffocated, drowned.*

*Electricity, crushing weights, clubs, pliers, razorblades, ropes, human excrement, ice, fire, sand, venomous creatures*

*— the system in its perfection includes them all.*

 *In my bakery, during the occupation, I had served members of the other Army. Officers, they had a taste for my ciabatta. Then too there was my daughter's arrest.*

 *This is how it happened that I was brought to those rooms where the lights are always buzzing.*

 *The walls inside are white. So too is the floor — but for the stains.*

 *The interrogators — have I mentioned? — are white-clad, white-shoed, white-gloved. This is intended, I suppose, to heighten the shock upon seeing the first of the blood.*

 *As I say, though, it's common business. I was not special — not in the way they suspected, nor in my treatment.*

 *Anyway, the dead are not interested in blame.*


*Within the hour the first hungry ones, going by, stop long enough to rifle my pockets. My pockets, of course, were emptied by the soldiers upon my arrest four days ago, and I am shoeless. Still, my body is turned about, searched again and again — eleven times by nightfall.*

 *In the night, under curfew, the dogs come to bathe the body with their tongues, a lone cur at first, and within a half-hour a small pack. Sniffing, nudging, they are assiduous, soon nibbling into the deeper wounds about wrists and neck. They've been at it a few hours when a burst of glass scatters them.*

 *Someone has thrown a bottle — then come rocks.*

 *The dogs, yelping, retreat down the road.*

 *And here from the shadows comes a figure in uniform, gun strapped upright at one shoulder. He moves hurriedly along the sidewalk, keeping close to the wall. He has a torchlight. He clicks it on and trains it on my body's face. Light, light in those eyes again.*

*But I am in the dark, out here beside dead man and soldier in the dark. The soldier kneels and I think he means like all the others to rummage pockets and tear at clothes — but no. From his own pocket he takes a cloth and after wetting this some with his spittle, and after brushing back the hair that's fallen there begins to dab at my face. Ever so carefully, with the patience of a nurse, he sponges off the crusted blood, all the while shooting glances over his shoulder and up and down the street.*

*And finally, having wiped the eyes and nose down to black clots and bruises, he sits back on his heels, breathing. Then, conclusively, he whispers my name.*

*Umberto.*

*Though I do not know him, he knows me. He was not one of my torturers. Has he come to atone nonetheless?*

*He doesn't linger, his glance still restless. He touches one of the dead and bloody hands, then he's up and scurrying.*

*Who is he? I'll go with him and find out. And so we leave the body where it lies and I trail him through shadows, not even a shadow myself.*

*They take you out of time.*

*In the small white blindingly lit rooms there are no clocks, no windows. Their system wants to teach you that time, which you thought of as adversary, was your friend all along. What's brutal is timelessness — not knowing an hour from a day, a day from a week. To be bound to time is a blessing, a mercy. To say to oneself, These beatings are a matter of hours, days, the time will pass and they will cease.*

*It's another one of the system's flaws that this logic can only collapse in upon itself. For the brutality in the white rooms comes to a point at which the real mercy, the real blessing, can only be death. True timelessness.*

*Knowing nothing, you can give them nothing. While they, intending to punish you, simply give you mercy. The sole accomplishment is now the thing no one intended at the start. Or maybe they intended it all along. The Army has never prized clemency.*

I know where he's going. This is the way to my sector. Perhaps he was a neighbor? But then would I not remember him?

He stays to the wall, in shadow wherever possible. He pauses at many places along the way, listening.

The quarters through which we pass are very quiet, all the windows blacked. In the north-south streets we move in low copper moonlight, and he hurries for the darkness every time.

At Godran Square there's a patrol, a few Army tents, much rumbling of tanks. It must be crossed but he hesitates, checking his shoulder constantly.

That's just me, I murmur. Umberto.

But I fail to make myself heard. Anyway, he doesn't respond.

Now he's backtracked to an alleyway and in the blackness he squats and checks a handgun, snapping it open and shut again. It takes a second or two at most and then, satisfied, he's out in the street, pacing steadily, not fast, toward the *square. He turns along the south edge of the square and now we're out in plain view and other soldiers are passing along this sidewalk. At the east side of the square behind us, two or three tanks make rounds.*

*My soldier slows. From his trench coat breast pocket he fishes a cigarette and lighter, stopping a moment to light up. Smoking, he proceeds in a swagger along the square. We turn the corner along the west side.*

*Hey! A passing solider blocks our path.*

*But he only wants a smoke.*

*Thanks.*

*My soldier returns the lighter to a pocket — his thigh pocket this time, where the ready gun is hidden. His hand remains in this pocket as he surveys the square.*

*Then we are at the north side, my sector, and again he is hastening through shadows. He knows the way.*

*At my bakery door, he cups his hands to look in the windows. They are all blacked. He turns about to scan the street in both directions, draws a breath, then raps at the door.*

*The noise rattles up and down the empty lane.*

*He waits, unnerved.*

*They are in there, I murmur. It will take them a moment, they'll be frightened.*

*He raps again and this time calls out: Army!*

*The blacking shifts in the window of the apartment next door, an old woman's face appears in the gap.*

*That's old Estella, my neighbor.*

*He sends her a savage wave and she hides again.*

*At last the latch inside my door is turning, and my wife peeks out.*

*The soldier bends and whispers, Umberto is dead. The Army complex, Topa Precinct. I am sorry. He turns to go.*

*My wife's appalled face darts forth. Who are you?*

*Josepha's friend, he whispers, and begins to cut away around the corner.*

*But Josepha, says my wife, confused and beginning to cry, Josepha is also dead.*

*The soldier halts. Dead?*

*She was detained first. Don't you know? It was you that did it — the Army, your comrades. Now you've killed them both!*

*She is sobbing.*

*The soldier tarries, looking alarmed. I … I did? He stops himself.*

*They are gone, my wife is crying, gone!*

*The soldier glances up the street again. I am sorry, he repeats, and he vanishes.*

*I remain with my grief-shocked wife.*

*But darling, darling, I am here.*

. . .

# 4.

# Works Lost :
## The Private Papers
## of G. P. Leed

Janos Lavin, in his painting "The Lido" (late 1952/early 1953) paints real human swimmers in action while, in the background on shore, a wall of mosaic art depicts figures also swimming. Privately he described the work's effect as consisting of the contrast between movement "resolved" and movement "that is just becoming. ...The drawing on the tiles is like a mask or cast from which the actual figures have broken free."

This new book of mine, I see, will be identically structured. Two parts: the cast and the body from which it is made.

*

The work consists mostly of waiting, of letting the material grow under your hands.

*

Think of Giotto's "Annunciation" in the Capella Scrovegni, up on the arches of the proscenium before the apse. On the left arch: the angel. Clear across on the right arch: the Virgin. But Giotto unites them by the graceful flowing of a piece of the angel's robe. Our eye follows the robe as it reaches toward her, and the traveling of the eye reinforces the realness of the moment, its immediacy. Time transpires as the eye goes across, time adding its movement to the image, unlocking the image, unfreezing it, so that the image itself moves through time. It's a kind of ingenious "motion picture," a unity of parts in concert.

*

Today, on a street corner a few blocks from here, I saw
a man bent over spitting out his own teeth.

*

On the curb in front of one of the houses halfway down
this block, a woman sits with two small children, a boy
and a girl. The children's hair is long and tangled, the
palms of their hands are nearly black with grime. They
are malnourished, their bellies swell as if with great
tumors. They've been sitting there, these three, for two
days. This morning, with the Doctor's blessing, I
brought them a pitcher of milk, a bag of sliced bread.

 The hands of the hollow-eyed mother are deep as
cups, emptier than empty.

*

Next day. Mother and children are gone. I see that my
little gift was taken to mean that they should go away.
Or, it occurs to me, maybe someone took them in.
When I say so to the Doctor, though, he tells me no,
they're gone. Who knows where?

*

Doesn't the sheet of paper grow infinitesimally heavier
with each word written upon it? Doesn't each thought
acquire greater substance and mass through the process
of writing, its embodiment in ink?

 There <u>is</u> weight to this work, it is not all abstraction
and philosophy — or worse, mere cogitation. No,
mustn't be. What makes the work real is that it can be
added to a scale, hung in actual balance. Working,

reading, you seek an authentic tug, as a hand that holds an object is pulled toward the ground.

Always we are disembodied, atomized, moving at light speed through some wire or other. Good work can soar at speed too, by all means. But we also want gravity — a footing in ourselves, or, one at a time, in each other.

*

Kasden writes. He mentions Cedric's involvement in the production of a film — an adaptation of a work first published in *Green Window* years ago. Would I care to visit the film set?

*

Rosetta came today — a reunion of kinds. A long time since I've been able to pay — and now, living here, I must cover her train fare from the capital. But yes, I managed to secure this one further visit at least. Ah, Rosetta, the baker's daughter! Her hands are scarred with many burns suffered in her youth. And they are strong hands, long practiced in the turning and kneading of dough, the fingers lithe and firm. I touched the smooth raised scars, telling her, "Rosetta, you're a nourisher! A maker and bringer of the bread of life. I am grateful to every burn for everything it's taught you." Having learned so well, she's a teacher. That's her true profession. As with all great teachers, her knowledge is a pure overflowing and imparting to every man she touches. Her sincerity humbles. She's no cynic or mercenary. We lay beside each other remembering our other times, enumerating slowly and paying each its

*167*

homage. A ceremony. Limbs entwined, we meditated upon our history, the intimate chronicle our bodies have written over years. Even in a world of data it is only the human body that knows how to remember.

Rosetta, with you there is no taking of accounts, no mere information, no algorithm. The data columns of the age have come to subdivide people's beds. The body's sweat is presumed to be pixelated, love held to be transactional in nature. In you though, Rosetta: all the generosity and memory of the baker's art!

*It is not known where Leed acquired the funds for this visit. Perhaps from his very infrequent freelance work, perhaps by loan.—Ed.*

*

"Philosophy is really homesickness: the wish to be everywhere at home." —Novalis

*Reference unknown.—Ed.*

*

To the movie set with Kasden today. I admit that I went in a spirit of superior amusement, prepared to find a mass display of self-importance. Well, I wasn't disappointed.

A film set is a perfect microcosm of all our delusional feudal hierarchies. Even the arrogance of court servants toward their brothers in the peasantry is replicated there. The gaffes, gophers, grips, etc. — all industrial peons themselves — are as haughty as imaginable to the non-initiated visitor. We were constantly in somebody's way. Even while made to stand in the corner we understood through signs and signals that at the first misstep our privileges could be swiftly revoked. The scorn is so prodigious it hangs in the set like steam, coating everyone.

It is understood — no, it's wholly taken for granted — that this industry with its elaborate backdrops, lavish costumes, unimpeachable realism, and unlimited powers of magic and spectacle, is the ultimate end and aim of all 'cultural production.' <u>All</u> books, naturally, exist in the ardent wish for the apotheosis of adaptation. A work of narrative, until it's translated to film, has failed to have its potential properly exploited. What could be more urgent, more culturally relevant, than the making of a movie?

The set was massive, constructed with impressive attention to detail inside a gargantuan warehouse. Cedric, affable as ever, walked us through the rooms of the faux house during a filming break. He works as a kind of associate producer on the project. His main responsibility, he said, is to serve as liaison between the author and the production team. "Really," he murmured, "I'm their one-man author placation service. Suppress all the author's concerns while pretending to address them, that sort of thing." The absurdity not lost upon him, he bugged out his eyes.

We stood a minute or two in each of the fake rooms admiring the props. The book, a massive popular success, is the story of a half-mad, larger-than-life writer — his war adventures, sexual conquests, alcoholism, and suicide. An ideal rendition of the artist for our times, so perfectly does he embody the need to trivialize, marginalize, and dismiss the creative worker as a tragic clown, irredeemable eccentric, social degenerate, etc. In the room of the set replicating the protagonist's study, we examined the desk populated with all the requisite trappings: a mess of papers and wine-stained notebooks, a crushed beer can, an ashtray overflowing with butts, a snub-nose revolver employed casually as paperweight, a dried red rose, a shadeless lamp (the dome of the naked bulb blackened), a money-clip thick with a wad of dollars, a smudged Pulitzer trophy adorned with a red satin garter, and enthroned amid this heap of detritus, the central hulking oddity, totem of the anachronistic crank: a manual typewriter.

"They go all out, don't they?" said Cedric.

Each of us saw clearly what was underway here. What could we do but smile?

A little later we stood back and watched the filming of a scene. The writer and his mistress, following the prior scene's rabid lovemaking, get in an argument. Kasden and I were outside the set, facing the bare plywood exterior of the room where the actors argued, but on a nearby monitor we could see what the camera was seeing inside. The writer, shirtless and hirsute, perches on the edge of his desk fumbling with cigarette and lighter. Beyond him in the frame is his tousled lover, wearing only a limp silken nightie. At her back is the equally tousled bed. They argue on. The writer, mumbling, manages to light his cigarette. From my place on the studio floor, outside the set walls, I watched the puffs of smoke rise through the lighting grid and upward into the gaping heights of the warehouse. This world of the movies has no top to its head.

*

"I don't know whether other authors experience what I do: a feeling that they may be writing a secret language that nobody else will be able to interpret."— Patrick White to Ben Heubsch, 1954
*White & Heubsch: unknown persons.—Ed.*

*

Rendered, by the work of imagination, outcast and honoree. Both.

*

-Your countrymen. Have you abandoned them?
-No. They are everywhere.
-Everywhere?
-Everywhere, yes.
-Even those what may gun you down tomorrow?
-Yes, sadly even those.

*

Dream: on a journey, trying to get somewhere. Had no car, lost my one suitcase, insufficiently dressed. Got soaked in a sudden downpour and ended up in a train station waiting room, in line, hoping to board.

Station personnel were questioning all passengers. My soaked condition, my lack of luggage, and all my obvious anachronism made me the object of their special attention. I stood before a table where a woman questioned me at length. Behind me, the long line of would-be passengers listened in, all delayed by my poor performance.

*Question:* Occupation?

I hesitated, but I did say "writer."

*Question:* What does the smell of warm, somewhat ripped velvet remind you of?

For this I could bring to mind absolutely zero associations. The woman offered to blindfold me, saying, "Sometimes it helps." I declined, certain that handcuffs would follow. She waited, relentlessly patient, for my answer. Clearly, the longer I delayed on any one answer the more prolonged and intensive the line of questioning would be. The lady went away for a moment, then came back, and I said lamely, "I've thought of something. My mother's stockings. The musty smell of the top drawer where she kept them."

*Question:* Capricorn, Sagittarius, Aries, blank.

But I had never memorized the Zodiac, I had no idea. I felt my scanty education keenly.

I believe I was led to another room. Anyway I was soon facing another inquisitor.

"Bibliomancy," said this other woman, and then waited, studying me.

"Yes," I answered. "What it means of course is foretelling the future by consulting at random the pages of a book."

She made reference to the fact that I had no luggage. Confirmed.

She then pointed out that I had been observed, earlier the same day, walking up and down the town sidewalk with a 12-inch breadknife in hand.

I recalled the situation to which she referred and immediately what had seemed perfectly normal behavior to me at the time now seemed utterly bizarre and unjustifiable.

And yet I could still recall the logic that had guided my behavior, so I relied upon this as explanation. It was all I could do.

I'd been walking along the sidewalk, I explained, when the limb of a medium-sized tree had projected itself into my face, requiring that I duck and swerve in order to continue along my way. This I did and then, a moment later along the sidewalk, in a small drawer beside a parking meter, I found the bread knife. It looked sufficiently sharp, its serrated blade in fact quite saw-like, so I doubled back with the knife in hand to perform the public service of removing the offending tree limb. This was managed easily enough — the limb was not very thick, the wood rather soft. Then I'd noticed a place in the center of the tree, at the branching of its trunk, where conceivably a person could lean comfortably and take in a view of the street. Except, at the moment a number of medium-sized twigs obscured the view. So I set about sawing off these twigs one by one. Sure enough, with the job done the view from that spot was very pleasant. I leaned there a while, admiring. Then, realizing I ought to be getting to the station, I headed along the street again. I'd gone a few blocks when it occurred to me that I still held the breadknife. This must have been, admittedly, a strange sight. It was one thing for a man to be putting the knife to good use as a saw in grooming a municipal tree. To carry it around without any explicit purpose was downright strange. Some people were, I noticed, observing me with a little alarm. I couldn't recall how I rid myself of the knife, only that the next thing I knew I was at the station.

Their questioning continued.

I awoke.

*

"Those who more and more must make all out of the privacy of their thought."—Yeats
*Yeats: unknown personage.—Ed.*

*

The father's body was found today in a ravine. Four days the man wandered in the forest, the Doctor tells me, then followed a freezing creek until succumbing to hypothermia, exhaustion. The place they found him was within a mile of his family's vehicle as the crow flies.

*

Despite the twelve million people in the Territory, there is very little civilization to be had. What you have instead, despite all so-called advancements, is nature — always vaster, always in contention with the abstracted aims of the little crowds. Only nature ever comes near a point of apotheosis. Only nature, strangely enough, has any power.

*

Jacketed figures stepping from sidewalks, leaning into traffic, hoping to spot the bus on its way.

*174*

\*

We are always homesick.

\*

-Who seeks entry here?

-I am His Majesty Emperor of Austria King of
Hungary.

-I know him not, who seeks entry?

-I am Emperor, Apostolic King of Hungary, King of
Bohemia, Dalmatia, Croatia, Slavonia, Galicia,
Lodomeria, Illyria, Jerusalem, Archduke of Austria,
Grand-Prince of Transylvania, Grand Duke of Tuscany
and Krakow, Duke of Lorraine, Salzburg, Styria,
Carinthia, and Carniola.

-I know him not, who seeks entry here?

-A humble sinner, who begs God's mercy.

Following enactment of this dialogue, the Kaiser's
coffin would enter the Church of the Capuccins in
Vienna.

\*

In the vast royal crypt, Josef II's copper casket stood
unassumingly in a corner, just outside the vaulted room
where his mother Maria Theresia's enormous
monument loomed enwrought with acanthus leaves,
angels, and trumpets. Without dais or ornamentation,
the son's container bore a green algaeic patina. Some of
its edges, brittled over time, had begun to crack. Near it
a notice was posted, soliciting the public for donations
to aid restoration and maintenance. This was Mozart's
king.

How many caskets down there — rows upon rows,

room after room! Innumerable branches of the
Habsburg family tree. These royal births. These
honored interments. That obscurity.

*

The corridors of the house where Franz Schubert died,
age 30. Narrow stairwell, bare stone stairs, stucco
peeling from the walls, a dark musty odor. I didn't want
to pay the fee to go inside the actual sad apartment.
One could do this, though. If one wished, one could buy
a ticket and stand in the rooms, wonder how the
furniture might have been configured on that day,
perhaps look out the windows considering the value of
a good view, how consoling a better one than this
might have been, remembering the price of such things.

"Wenn es stimmt, daß Applaus das Brot des
Künstlers ist, hätte Franz Schubert wohl verhungern
müssen." If it's true that applause is the bread of artists,
then Franz Schubert must have been extremely hungry.
*Schubert: unknown personage.—Ed.*

*

The scratch and tap of a crow's feet on the copper
weathervane.

*

Thick fog this morning, hardly diminished by
afternoon. I went out early for a walk, a few hours'
diversion. The fog soaks up the color of every leaf and
grass blade and hides it away in some innermost
chamber like a sponge. It is surrendering weather — it
blots out all horizon, leaves you nothing but the present
moment.

*176*

\*

Here and there in the park, the lawn lay netted with
conical gossamers like shrunken cyclones.

\*

Dailiness: the soothing beauty of it. At times it seems
full of reassurance, of affirmation, of blessedness, like a
picture by Chardin. The puddles in the pavement,
where the potholes and rough surfaces are. Some days
they have meant dejection. Today they seemed worthy
of a passing admiration, so humbly picturesque, so
familiar — and comely for being so.
*Chardin: French still-life artist of the 18th-century.—Ed.*

\*

"Absolute outsideness forever eludes us." —Robert
Frost
*Robert Frost: American poet. Works lost. —Ed.*

\*

First memory (and why should it visit me now, so
suddenly?): The sight of two ceiling beams coming
together in a vaulted triangular place. Sunlight on
white plaster and wood. The knowledge, very pure and
certain, that the day is Sunday.

\*

Another: the fragrance of fresh-cut lemons, and the
lemon tree from which you would pluck bees by the
wings, in fearless wonder, and never get stung.

\*

Memory is like being at great altitude above a sea.
When seen from such height, the motions of the water
appear to freeze.

A dropping of guards. A bending and subverting of
one's own assumptions. A readiness to yield, give
ground, be transformed. Altruism as virtue (though it
be labeled pretense by those who move in realms where
such a thing is impossible or passé).

What is necessary in this work is to put yourself on
the line. It is hard. It is dangerous. But <u>this</u> is the task.
Idiosyncrasy can only come honestly, not by pushes or
shouts. It comes, most often, with pangs of humility. A
willingness to be embarrassed. Or, nowadays, to be all
but disappeared.

*

"What concerns me is that man, unable to articulate, to
express himself adequately, reverts to action. Since the
vocabulary of action is limited, as it were, to his body,
he is bound to act violently, extending his vocabulary
with a weapon where there should have been an
adjective."—Joseph Brodsky
*Reference unknown.—Ed.*

*

Beauty: not an <u>effect</u>; not achieved by contrivance or
technique; not a quality one can struggle toward; not an
end for which one may devise a means. Not this, not
this.

1) Beauty is <u>resonance</u>, indivisible, organic,
unfakeable. An experience.

2) Beauty does not curtsy and cannot be coaxed.

3) Beauty may result from labor, but <u>not because</u> the
artist has labored for beautiful effect.

4) Beauty, as a state, relates intrinsically to the devoted state of the artist, but one is powerless to craft beauty directly from the clay of dedication.

5) One has the means, at most, to create conditions propitious to the <u>emergence</u> of beauty. The thing itself one cannot create directly, but one may let it come forth.

*

"Where there is form there can be empathy. It must surprise us, working its effect before we have become conscious of its presence."—Herbert Read
*Read: unknown personage.—Ed.*

*

The wonderful, delusional midpoint of a work-in-progress. All energies are rallied and all confidence in place, unassailable. You can't imagine stopping, you can hardly remember ever having been without the work at hand. Haven't you always lived this way? This is existence!

*

<u>Fiction</u> n. from FICTILE: made of earth or clay by a potter.

↓        ↓        ↓

The whole process a material, physical one, a tactile handling and shaping of elemental substances. The single consciousness, earthborn and rendered by hand. The clay is the body and mind, our humanity. The water with which the potter makes it pliable is language. The wheel upon which he spins it is the page.

The kiln that fires it is quietude, solitude, time — and the <u>intuition</u> these engender.

How different, all this, from the dream of the technologist.

*

"It comes from life but it is not life. It is something else. It is a poem of life. ... There comes a time in life when you realize that everything is a dream. Only those things that have been written down have any possibility of being real. That's all that exists in the end: what's been written down."—James Salter
*Reference unknown.—Ed.*

*

I've been borrowing two books from Kasden's shop. From one of them, an ancient little paperback, a small tri-folded brochure fluttered out. Brittle paper, brown at its edges, it shows a man in bow tie and tortoiseshell glasses smiling benignly. Beside his picture, large type inquires: "DO YOU HAVE A RESTLESS URGE TO WRITE? IF YOU DO, HERE IS AN OPPORTUNITY FOR YOU TO TAKE THE FIRST IMPORTANT STEP TO SUCCESS IN WRITING." Inside the tract you read the following: "Have your writing tested by a group of America's most successful authors. This is the same Test thousands of men and women have already taken. It has started many on the road to success in writing. Send for the Famous Writers Aptitude Test. Simply mail the postcard below. With the Test, you will receive a 48-page Famous Writers School brochure. Your test will be graded by a member of our staff. If you test well — or offer other

*180*

evidence of writing aptitude, you may enroll. However, there is no obligation to do so. Find out if you have talent worth developing!"

The postcard in this particular brochure was never detached. In that there is retrospective comfort of a kind. What would happen if I sent it in, all this time later?

*

"As bourgeois society increasingly destroys and corrupts the general, popular creative spirit, the experience of imaginative creation becomes rarer and rarer till in the end people think there is some magical secret for creativity." —Janos Lavin

*

Bewildering, the widely exhibited urge to become exceptional — but only by the most conventional means. 'Aptitude,' 'skillset,' 'success,' 'fame.' The terms by themselves are innocent enough. Once applied as a terminology they become insidious. Used as inroads to artistic life, they are — worse than useless — distorting.

*

Dear Kasden,
I'm reading the novel you lent me, and of course you were right, every page is a pleasure. The deeper I proceed, the more pressing the question becomes: Who is this author, this Norah ------ ? No one knows her, naturally. Today, at a post office terminal, I dared to enter her name in the Network. To tell the truth, I half feared she'd come up dead. As it happens, she resides in

181

East-Northwest Territory, not all that far from you or me. I think we should track her down. Sure, it's been 20 years since this novel, but I'd venture she's writing yet. A gift like hers, there's no helping it probably. And she may need books. Think how <u>we</u> need them.

Adventure! What say you?

—G

*This letter was recovered secretly from Market Optimization Bureau files.—Ed.*

\*

Remembering today, for no particular reason, a painting by William Coldstream called "Studio Interior." The whole canvas is a shadowy brown wash. In a bare room an artist confronts one of his creations, a bust. And the bust is realer, more featured, than its maker. It has been given a face. Where the artist's own face should be, though, there is only blank surface. The man himself is faceless.

\*

Art abhors the authoritative.

\*

The length of the line before the carriage return, those intervals between the chime of the bell, they're essentially human in dimension, being of a duration conducive to good breathing. Thus the typewriter engenders a naturally rhythmic use of each line, a fine (unconscious) attunement in each sentence.

By contrast, a digital terminal disregards such intervals, such rhythm, in favor of the unstructured infinity of the screen. Thus the choppy, awkward, insistently non-sensual sentences all around us. Language born outside of the body. Language in abject surrender to a culture of data.

*

The staccato whistling made by ducks flapping overhead.

*

We are each only <u>ourselves</u>, however rampant the desire to upload and exponentialize individual identity. There is only consciousness <u>singular</u>, self-contained. A myriad selves. Spheres that may touch, at most, other spheres. The project of literature is this, embodied in the singular selves — the revolving spheres — of every sentence.

Yet today we believe, and our writers have come to believe, too much in a <u>social</u> consciousness, a thing collective in nature, made up of the mass, larger itself than the sum of its parts. Such a thing does not exist. A literature seeking to capture it is a literature predicated on falsity, the dreams of the technologist.

*

A literature preoccupied with language, a work that presumes to consist of sentences, is a work presumed to have little to say. What is most esteemed is documentation, line after line dashed off in the hurry to encyclopediate the national life and self (neither of which truly exist). Language that lingers appears to ignore the imperative to catalog, to gather up. A beautiful sentence is viewed with suspicion, the book consisting of sentences brushed aside, Irrelevant. The writer has declined the beck and call of Ambition — so it's believed.

The bias is strong. It permeates the culture. It will soon be beyond us, if it isn't already, to recognize the infinite capacity of a line as carrier of, vessel for, doorway to — consciousness. And what else is this world — this world that so wants witnessing — made of but consciousness? To render consciousness in a sentence, in language, in the all-seeing eye of a fully created line, <u>this</u> is to render the world.

*

The technologist's syllogism:

The human brain appears to function by electrical signals and obviously stores information;

A computer functions by electrical signals and stores information;

A computer's functions are easily reducible to mathematical functions;

A computer is a kind of brain;

Therefore a brain is a computer, equally reducible by mathematics!

Therefore a computer programmer can create a human brain!

Therefore the Network, being comprised of computer signals, will eventually be comprised of an infinite number of replicated brains!

Therefore the Network will inevitably exhibit consciousness and become a sentient identity!

*

Oh but consider the mysterious workings of memory,

which consist of so much more that the mere retrieval of data. The mind of man, consciousness itself, is <u>irreducible</u> — unlike the mathematical functions of a machine. Here the illusion collapses.

*

"Biologically speaking, man is a moderately gregarious, not a completely social animal — a creature more like a wolf, let us say, or an elephant, than like a bee or an ant. … However hard they try, men cannot create a social organism, they can only create an organization. In the process of trying to create an organism they will merely create a totalitarian despotism." —Aldous Huxley *Reference unknown.—Ed.*

*

Quis custodiet custodes?

*

A thing is not really what we call it. Spoken language is a <u>representation</u> of the thing, <u>momentarily</u> captured in <u>voice</u>.

Writing is, in turn, a representation of speech, <u>durably</u> captured in <u>print</u>.

Electronic text is merely a representation of writing, <u>momentarily</u> captured <u>in electronic signals</u> — an image that appears or vanishes at the press of a button, depending on electrical supply. The most abstract and unstable by far. A facsimile of a facsimile.

*

With Kasden to the capital yesterday, in search of Norah ------'s address. It was easy enough to find. We were standing at the door within an hour of our arrival.

Not so good a neighborhood, naturally, but anyway even the good ones aren't much better, the notion of neighborhood having all but left us. We knocked and a voice answered, sounding small and far away. We were kept on the step talking through the door for several minutes. Finally our assurances had their effect — no, we were not Bureau agents — and the door was opened. Standing before us was a shrunken old woman, four and a half feet tall at most. She wore a knitted crimson cardigan done up with great wooden medallions for buttons, a fleece muffler, and a blue and yellow ski cap. In her smallness, her age, and the spring-like brightness of the wide blue eyes in her drooping face, she was utterly gnomic. I'd failed, in reading her novel and glancing at the photo on its jacket, to imagine how old she would be now. The book's vivacity had fixed its author in time, though that time was 30 years ago. And here she was.

She did not invite us in. We told her a little about ourselves, the journey we'd taken to find her, how much her novel had meant to us. She listened, somewhat guardedly. Only when Kasden reached into his coat and brought out her book did something give way. The hint of a smile quivered across her face.

"I thought ... I thought they'd all been Processed!" she said in disbelief.

"Not all," said Kasden, handing her the copy.

Soon we were inside her disastrous apartment and she was skittering around clearing off a few places to sit. There were only two or three rooms and a kitchen.

Debris lay everywhere in mounds and trails: moldering
cardboard boxes, mousetraps, plastic wrappers, toppled
lamps, articles of clothing, stray hardware, a dozen or
so half-melted candles. She found two broken chairs,
the cane seats punched through. Kasden and I balanced
on the rims of these while Norah sat atop a wobbling
end table. A gray feeble light seeped in through an
aluminum-framed window. Behind Norah, in the little
passage leading to the bedroom, ceiling water dittered
into a mop bucket on the floor. We talked, and all the
while she kept the book in her hands. There was a kind
of disbelief — a starved faith — in the way her fingers
clasped it. She apologized for the chill. Electric heating,
she explained, but the power has been off for years. She
was sorry she couldn't offer a warm drink but she
rations the stove gas very carefully. She is the
building's landlord, ekes out a life that way — her
tenants are largely transients, fugitives, the mortally ill.
Some she shelters strictly as charity, others she barters
with or they pay what little they can. She used to be a
librarian in the central library downtown. Had a desk in
the closed stacks, and it was there, after hours for five
or six years, that she sat writing the novel. The library
was still a landmark in those days — though already
funding was in ever-deepening jeopardy. Its vast
holdings were still a point of municipal pride and the
palatial structure itself drew gawking visitors from all
territories. Norah, in the glow of her desk lamp after
hours, dreamed and worked at her peculiar pages. All
the time, she said, she drew strength from the miles and

miles of packed shelves coiling through the rooms on the library's multiple floors. When blocked or beginning to lose heart, she got up and wandered the stacks. All hours of night, the city's gleam entered through the arches of the countless windows and the spines of books in their protective Mylar wrappers glittered. She had only to take one down and open it to gain back her strength, to remember what she was about. It was a year or two after the novel's publication that Network Preeminence took hold and the collections were liquidated for Processing, the library itself eventually demolished. She's been biding her time in that apartment ever since. Early on, the Bureau paid its calls. But somewhere along the line they managed to verify that she had ceased writing, and now their visits are only occasional, concerned in the main with her transmission quotas, though even that is just bureaucratic formality. She owns no device and they know it, but they threaten her with little more than their nuisance.

It's true, she is not writing anymore. Though the circumstances of her life indicate defeat, though she seems wary, tired, habitually rather glum, still there's a kind of stoic glint about her. She sees the shame of all that has happened, she could wish it was otherwise, but she is busy surviving — she has no patience for tragedy. Her life is a shrug, a getting-on-with-it. She seems to say, 'Isn't any fate, any destiny, any life absurd when considered as our only one? — the expense of a hundred others at which it must come?' But she is not a nihilist. A person like Norah can be encouraged.

"We wanted to know," we told her, "if you would like to have books again."

All at once her eyes were sparkling.

We said, "We are resisters and we'd like to have you for a contact. We want you to keep writing."

She was still clutching her book. And we let her keep it as we took our leave. Of course. What book, at this late turning-point, could she need more than her own?

It's true. Life can be lived in this work. You can live for this.

*

PREMISE:

1) Neuroplasticity and the social circuitry of the Network are analogous phenomena.

2) The Network has become in a real sense the societal brain.

3) The science of neuroplasticity holds that the individual can change his/her own behavior and thus consciously reshape the cellular function of his/her brain for the better. This however is not easy once deleterious behavior has become ingrained (foreshortened attention spans, etc.).

4) Changing ingrained societal behaviors — as in working to reshape the societal brain as it manifests through the Network — is magnitudinously harder than the already hard task of changing individual behavior.

5) This is the moral of much dystopian literature.

6) If one is concerned about the ways the Network and related digital technologies have changed individual and societal brain function; if one feels, intuitively, the value in questioning such qualitative change; if one sees the benefits of skepticism when confronted with the utopian claims of the technocracy, then one may try — as an <u>individual</u> wholly capable of modifying <u>his/her own behavior</u> — to resist.

<u>PROPOSAL:</u>

7) I, a single neuron in the societal brain, refuse to be rewired.

8) I dread and resist the 'digital renaissance,' the effects of which are: disempowerment of the individual, fragmentation, algorithmic and statistical hegemony, total corporate conquest, the annihilation of privacy, the supremacy of advertising, the wholesale dependency on seductive machines, the furtherance of the new despotism and of tyrannical organizations, etc., etc.

9) I lay down my weapons and walk away.

*

Venetian glassblowers of the 13th-century who carried their trade secrets abroad were guaranteed by edict of the Doge to be hunted down by henchmen and murdered.

*

The two makers of the famous astrological clock in the Piazza San Marco were 'officially blinded to prevent them making another for somebody else.'

*

The system, as presently structured, ministers to our fear of the cave man — a horror of the wild, un-Networked, and likely un-Networkable corners of the earth. The deep forests, remote mountains, and deserts where the non-technological persists, where Nature by its stately example, or by its bleak indifference to progress, seems counter-evolutionary.

Is there anything more frightful to people today than those shrieking wild men in the desert, stamping dusty feet in jubilation at the falling of airplanes half a world away — airplanes their fellow troglodytes brought down screaming, thanks to nothing more than boxcutters?

*

The desire for collective consciousness is natural in basis. Ironically, though, it is a desire best served by an art-form that reaffirms the value of singular consciousness. This will forever be our sole vessel of crossing over to something beyond ourselves, of understanding one another.

One consciousness at a time.

Most of the time we will be inescapably ourselves, but sometimes, through imagination, we may seem to become another.

We can never be the whole, or ourselves within the whole, for the whole as such does not exist.

*

"The illusory nature of freedoms not based on personal responsibility."—Havel

[Vaclav] Havel: 20th-century Czech playwright, dissident,

*and first President of the Czech Republic. Several of his powerful resistance writings, born in samizdat, endure in samizdat.—Ed.*

✳

"It only happens to one, though it may happen a million times to a million ones." —Alberto Manguel
*Reference unknown.—Ed.*

✳

"-There's a war. Where you're from becomes important. -I hate that. I hate that idea."
*Quotation unknown.—Ed.*

# 5.

# In Country

*She came to believe, even as they lay together, that he could not be trusted.*
   *What side are you on? she would ask him.*

Jude, still walking, could hear her voice even now.

*Shedding her clothes, in the end she could not shed the ideology. It gripped her, as she gripped the knife hidden beneath the mattress.*
   *And yet she did not kill him.*

He was walking in a ruined orchard. In many places the ground had been torn open. Everywhere the trees were black, many of them toppled, many more blasted to jagged stumps. These stood in scorched rows for miles. To pass among them was disorienting. In places Jude felt very tall, all but monstrous, in others he must clamber over fallen canopies, piles of ashen limbs and trunks.

   The orchard gave way to another, then still another, then he emerged in a sloping vineyard country, or the remains of one. The trellises were all fallen and the vines lay strewn like dried seawrack for miles.

Walking on for hours, he came to the mouth of a canyon. A great railroad bridge transected the sky, iron arches thrust over the gorge. Had some water, a massive river, poured down that chasm long before? Now it was dry, all clogged with rockfall, wooded in some places.

On the talus beneath the vaulted bridge Jude found himself standing in a sea of bone. Skulls, ribs, jaws, bits of arms or legs still clothed in tatters of cottonprint. Shattered skeletons amid the rocks. There were the remains of at least a hundred people here. They'd all fallen from the bridge above. Two years ago? Longer?

Someone had slowed the train. Someone opened the cargo doors. Someone pushed each prisoner. Again he looked up at the trestle. The sun winked to blind him.

And now something was glinting amid the bone and rock at his feet. Jude picked up a jagged fragment of wood. It was lacquered on one side — a mellow honey color — and there was the hint of a curve in it. Someone's hand tool had shaped it. Then Jude caught sight of the bare wooden neck jutting from the rocks. The ballad singer's instrument. Somebody, for all he could tell, had brought the instrument down sledge-like among the bones. Was it the singer himself? Or had singer and instrument both fallen, like the others before?

The instrument's pieces made a radius of many yards, all glinting softly like the piece in his hand. It was a dead sun. The bright debris had clattered as it flew and was dimming now. The strings were nowhere in sight. Like an abject flag or sapling the fretted neck stood.

What had become of the singer?

Jude slipped the fragment away in his pocket.

Stepping over the stones, he began to pick up skulls as he found them. His arms were soon full. The skulls he arranged at the base of the talus, fitted together in rows cheek by cheek and then stacked, gradually, until they made a cairn of kinds.

The black voids of the eyesockets stared out at the vineyard land in deathly chorus.

He was a few hours about the business. It seemed necessary before going on. Travelers after him would pause in this place, stand before the dumb white masonry of their own likeness, the hooded gaze of bone arranged in company decorative or commemorative.

*Who had ordered them so?*

# SKULLS

*Were you a mother?*

*Did you stand nights at a sleeping child's door, listening for breath beyond the gurgling of rain in gutters and spouts?*

*Were you a woodcarver? A birdkeeper? Librarian?*

*Were you clubfooted or a lover of dance?*

*Did you read the leaves in the cup of every guest?*

*Did you write and send letters and wait for letters back?*

*Did you tell yourself a story all your days?*

*Were you a swimmer, a gardener, a civil servant?*

*Did you read books in the evening, in a chair beside a window?*

*Did you walk daily to church, see the doctor but once every few years, put on hip boots and fish from the shallows?*

*Did you teach school?*

*Punch tickets?*

*Were you a healer?*

*A hunchback?*

*A lover of music?*

*Were you born where you lived?*

*Did you marry?*

*Could you remember earthquakes, storms, droughts, epidemics?*

*Did you ever count out coins and ration food?*

*Could you remember days of abundance?*
*Did you love dogs?*
*Did you watch morning's arrival over bodies of water?*
*Did you share a bed, a daily meal, a drinking glass?*
*Did you harbor jealousies?*
*Were you an architect, a glazier, a potter, a prostitute?*
*Did you know the loneliness of cities?*
*Did you fling your hat over borders?*
*Did you cultivate memories?*
*Were you a neighbor?*
*A baker?*
*Did friends sit to drink coffee at your table?*
*Did you write and send letters?*
*Did you observe the holy days?*
*Did you anoint your brow with ash?*
*Did you consider all the other gods?*
*Were you more often settled or moving?*
*Did you celebrate?*
*Did you despair?*
*Did you write and send letters?*

.   .   .

It was spring, or would be soon. The land said so. For all his cold, the rain, the earlier heat, Jude had nearly forgotten the laws of the calendar. That the world, having a life of its own, never ceased changing — however unchanging man could be.

He walked. Time was passing and he had been walking — for months? Longer? The war, the land it shaped, the signs and figures it drew in his being — it was a kind of eternity.

The land was very dry and he was thirsty. The sun, from somewhere remote above, leached the day's colors away, put a bony starkness in all he saw. Edges stood forth and seemed to hum.

His head was aching. His shadow bunched small at his feet.

As he walked along, the arcs of the waxen tree canopies, the camber of the land, the smallest pebbles underfoot, seemed to sharpen and soon everything was made of angles and points. A serrated vision. A country fitted together at a million small corners, like the panes of a church window. He felt himself a stained glass figure, his body knife-edged, cutting its way forward.

It seemed to him that somewhere in the frame, whether far beneath or high overhead, some arcane insignia bespoke his journey, the substance of his tale.

He couldn't see it — was it a sword or a holy dove?

He could feel, however, the presence of his own image duplicated at several places in the glass. He couldn't see these duplicates, but they were there, his recurring selves, each positioned differently, each depicting a turn in his story.

His legs had started to quiver. He was, he realized, walking very slowly. There was a stained glass olive tree just ahead off the road. He stopped beneath it, dropped his pilgrim sack, and lay down to rest.

He became the jagged figure of Jude Asleep.

For many days after he walked and slept along the road. In some of the trees there were olives, early fruits. Others gave forth little nuts like none he'd ever eaten. In one place he found a stand of anise weed.

He filled his sack as he went.

There were marshy spots amid the scrub brush, and he found that pawing the mossy topsoil away would sometimes reveal a meager seepage, puddles at which he could sip, prostrated and kissing the ground.


In time he entered a sun-washed country on a high plateau. It was strangely featured with earthen minarets and swollen mounds of soft volcanic stone. These ranged away for miles, now dromedary, now fingerlike, imitative of mountains but hardly even hills themselves, riddled or contorted carvings the wind had made.

In places amid this lunar terrain there were meager settlements. Houses, churches, places of commerce carved from the rock. The people of the region were peaceable, half-pagan, a gazing kind. They had burrowed here for centuries. It was rumored that they had built labyrinthine cities underground, a more elaborate civilization open only to them. They were not a warring people.

.  .  .

The days warmed. Nights, still cool, would find him
huddling in burrow or brush.

He kept walking. He made a way. He was shriveling,
but this was no concern. He was hardly aware of it. His
shadow winked ahead of him, a crescent upon the dusty
road.

He was going, still going. *The other way.* He'd heard
no news of the war, if it was still back there behind him.

He hadn't seen a mirror — in how long? He hardly
knew or remembered his own reflection.

He remembered bodies, Josepha, the word *Resistance.*

He was walking, a body himself. Moving upright,
onward, though more and more all planes and surfaces
reeled.

Nights were breathless, warming, and still.

Finally in the dark he collapsed along the road.

# ANY MAN, ANY WOMAN

*Did you know him well?*
*I thought I did, but then he thought the same of me.*
*Can anyone know such a man?*
*Can you know the sound of a spider's scurry?*
*He carried a staff.*
*He wore a large hat.*
*He always kept a pistol with him.*
*There was no pistol. He always went unarmed.*
*He was my killer.*
*He killed nobody.*
*There was blood all over him, not just his own.*
*I tried to kill him at the end, despite all we had shared.*
*He was a dead man.*
*He never struck back. Instead he helped me daub his blood off*
*my belly and breasts.*
*He was my brother.*
*My father.*
*He had no relations.*
*He understood hate.*
*The first time I fed him, he drank from a broken cup.*
*His name was Jude.*

*His name was Janos.*

*He had no name.*

*He'd forgotten his name.*

*He believed he must keep his name hidden forever.*

*He was traveling home.*

*He was running away.*

*He had no destination.*

*I betrayed him.*

*I was his brother.*

*I dreamt him up. He was never there at all.*

*They'd imprisoned him numerous times.*

*He'd have made a fine soldier.*

*He was a nihilist.*

*An anarchist.*

*A turncoat.*

*A mercenary.*

*I would have taught him the litanies.*

*He might have been a singer.*

*A healer.*

*A holy man.*

*Together we would have restored the cathedral, put the windows back pane by pane.*

*He might have worked for my father. We would have taught him to bake.*

*Had he any family of his own?*

*No.*

*Yes, and he lost them in the war.*

*No one has ever known.*

*In the end, yes.*

*He wore sturdy boots.*

*He grew thinner and thinner.*
*He could speak any language.*
*He hardly spoke at all.*
*He believed in the cause.*
*The Resistance was doomed and he gave it up.*
*In the end, we called him Jikan. The Silent One. It was a*
*name he gave to himself.*
*No, it was chosen for him.*
*He deserted.*
*He survived.*
*He forgot much of what came before.*
*Well, memory's mercy is in forgetting.*
*He forgot nothing.*

. . .

He heard a muffled voice and stirred.

*Rise up.*

Something scraped against his eyelids as they opened, a kind of crust.

He was peering through a wall. He was in a box of some kind. His vision was a slit, but there was a little light. The light was like a lid pressing in. He was breathing against it.

Then there was the figure of a man black against the light. Above him somehow. The man's head was a dark shield, rectangular. His words were flat and hollow. Rise up.

The man was masked, standing over him.

Jude breathed and tried to speak but his words were a croak.

Where was he? How long had he lain here?

The mask sank closer. The light branched behind it. The man and the mask were breathing with a curious heaviness.

You were dead. I woke you up.

Dead?

Yes. You died out on the road. You were walking a long time before you died.

His vision was coming back. He began to see the features of the mask now. There were small round holes for the eyes, a green line in place of the nose. Where the

mouth should be there was nothing. The mask looked
to be shaped of bark or balsa wood. It was stained or
painted black.

Do you feel this?

What?

Nothing, eh? I am touching your hands. Your
fingers are still very stiff. And this? I am touching your
feet now. No? Well, it takes time.

How long have I been here?

Here? Several days. But you were dead and it was
just your body here. Before that, out on the road, you
laid there a week probably. Maybe less. Time doesn't
matter much when you're dead.

What is this box? Am I in a coffin?

No coffin. No box. You are lying on the floor. You're
wearing the mask I made you.

Mask?

Yes, the mask is what brought you back. I only woke
you up.

Are you a doctor?

Some believe so. But as I say, the power is in the
mask. I only woke you.

Jude might have moved to sit up, but there could be
no moving yet. He'd been someplace very dark. His
mind was coming back, but the rest of him was still
there.

Where are we?

In my village. It is a small village.

Who are you?

A mask-maker. To some a shaman. To others an

onyx-carver. I collect the taxes also.

I'm very thirsty.

Yes, you must be. Here now, can you drink from this straw?

The mask-maker's voice drew closer and Jude felt a hand cradling the back of his head. His tongue, searching, touched the mask's interior, then the straw was tapping at his lips. He took hold and sucked and a brilliant icy coldness flooded his mouth. He only coughed a little, and drank the cup dry. He wanted more, he said, and asked that the mask come off to allow it.

That's enough just now, said the mask-maker. Now your body does the drinking and we wait.

Jude was feeling the wooden pressure of the mask. Would I die again if we took it off?

The mask is not everything, but yes, there's a danger.

And your mask?

Mine? Oh, I always wear one or another. I have no face, you see.

None at all?

His hands moved apart, a gesture of cancellation. None. The one I was born with was torn away.

In the war, you mean?

Yes. Shrapnel.

Were you a soldier?

No. Were you?

Jude lay thinking. I suppose I was.

On what side?

No side. Or…one or another.

The shaman shrugged, his mask remaining very still. Doesn't matter. There's always a side.

Jude lay. He believed he could hear a fire popping beyond the door. He believed a little sensation was seeping back into his fingers, his feet.

Do you miss your face?

I did, at first. The shock of losing it was very deep. But you learn to look for yourself elsewhere. Today I am this face. Tomorrow another.

Jude heard knuckles on wood. The shaman was rapping at the mask.

They fell quiet then. For a time Jude lay listening to the noises from the shaman's village outside. There seemed to be, from somewhere distant, the bleating of goats, the warped clatter of bells.

He drifted and slept.

*Where are you walking?*

The question woke him. Still he was lying on the mask-maker's floor.

He knew only that he was going east. *East*, he thought, but the mouth in his own mask would not open.

You will go on walking, said the shaman from somewhere in the shadows now, out of sight. You will walk for many seasons.

It was a kind of incantation. A prophecy or blessing, Jude couldn't tell.

Again he slept, and somewhere in dream or actual time the mask-maker went on.

*They have made a treaty. It is ended. You're done with death. I woke you up and the war is over. You will go home to your family now. Your house. Your people. You'll find them waiting.*

*No*, answered Jude, though the mask would say nothing. He had no people, he deserved no one's waiting, and for him the war would never end.


*They've made a treaty. It is over.*

*There are skeletons in the peaks, the jungles: of men, of lions. ... In burnt strata below, out of sight, lie old imperial capitals. ... In wilderness pools there are fish. In the high*

*whorls of trees are long-winged flies. These are parallel*
*kingdoms and time is real. We commit ourselves to its*
*carriage but a year never truly turns. … Death is a question*
*of soil, of blown leaves, of silence. …*

The voice kept talking.

# MASK-MAKER

*... Before nations, before maps and battles, there were many holy men.*

*We may have cities, villages — these are good, like family. But why must we have nations?*

*The holy men went higher and higher by their study. Many could change to lizards, to mice, to bees. The first masks came after that — the masks helped to teach this changing.*

*Becoming a dog, you could learn to see the world by its smell. You could smell all the feelings in the world.*

*Many could sit in a chair and train their thinking till they levitated or flew in the air. The masks were tools. It was a virtue to tear away your face for another's. It was understood this was necessary, natural. To dream inside the mask was a magical act of giving. I'm contained, and I contain.*

*To be dreamed well is a gift.*

*Then came maps and other powers and these studies began to vanish. Now very few can train their thinking like that. Instead of putting on the many faces of masks, people now make masks of their faces. The magic — the changing that the masks taught — is mostly lost. But only mostly.*

*In the walls of my house are no windows. I have hung my house with masks instead, and they are every window, every view, all things flowing together in the dark that lies behind.*

*I sand and shape wood, grind pigments and apply paint, collect feathers and affix them.*

*The war is over, the magic may come back.*

*Very gladly, from the mask's dark, would I look at the world through the eyes of a dog...*

. . .

He awoke to the sound of washing.

He could move his arms and legs. He found he could turn and push at the ground.

Then he was sitting up in the floor of the shaman's house. His head seemed to drift about his shoulders. He realized the mask had been removed. He was touching his face, breathing deep.

Had he really died before?

The house was very low, its walls all earthen, and several masks were hung about. Which of these was his?

From beyond the door, outside, there was a low spluttering noise.

He staggered up. He went and stood in the daylight of the dusty threshold, blinking.

Before him in the sun a small man was bent over at a clay basin, his bare back sinewy and brown. He was splashing his face.

The sunlight in the water was blinding. The droplets were sharp as diamonds. Hitting the dust, they seemed to chime.

Sensing his observer, the man at the basin stood upright, glittering wet.

Unmasked, he turned.

Jude, blinded anew, stared into the faceless head as if staring at the sun.

*He would walk for many seasons.*

*I tell myself the story now, and it is like another man's story…*

*In the autumn he walked through mountains.*

*By night sometimes he built lean-tos of pine boughs or just covered himself in leaves.*

*He shivered in the cold, was soaked by the rains, dried out in caves.*

*In the winter he found a village and was taken in, very weak, those months a hazy dream only hazily recalled. Faces of a woman, an old man, his caretakers, floating above his pallet on the floor. A cup of broth held gently to his lips. Snow swirling on panes of glass.*

*In the spring he went on, a saved man, grateful and uncomprehending.*

*There were many things to see and he saw them along his way.*

*In a very empty place, a small boy stood over a puddle. He was alone and did not raise his head. The sky was in the puddle and the land at his back was enormous.*

. . .

*In another place, a woman in rags moved along ringing the bells she held in each hand. Her knobby fists shook up and down, slow, a rhythm of great importance. She kept walking.*

*In a house one night — what house, he can't recall — a small girl watched him from behind a curtain. In her slant gaze there was no suspicion, no trust, only the calm vacancy of a girl's wish to look.*

*Elsewhere along the road a mad man traveled by donkey, the beast very scrawny and groaning all the way, the rider, his face all chapped and peeling, waving his arms, gesticulating, calling down curses and laughing.*

*A small village lay in a clearing, demolished, hurled over like a smashed sandcastle.*

*In the cold of a black night beside a pond, a prison-keeper and his prisoner sat stoking a weak fire. The prisoner was to be hanged the following morning, and the other man was duty-bound to do it. They were murmuring. They seemed to have reached an understanding, a means of passing the hours.*

*A club-footed man, moving laboriously along on two crutches, heaved himself up a hillside in the distance, growing smaller and smaller as he climbed, whistling at a mangy dog that ran ahead. Atop the hill he stood in the wind, seeming to feel the magnificence of his own silhouette.*

*Autumn brought him to the valley where they called him Jikan, Silent One, and here he settled. Apricots grew in this place, a fertile land.*

*He worked at the harvest. He helped raise some houses and was helped in raising his own.*

*Jikan, they would say. Always so silent.*

*They were a farming people and had lived in the valley for centuries. He wore the garments of their kind, observed their beliefs, learned the old dialect.*

*In the spring he married. The following spring his daughters were born: twins.*

*He became a man immersed in life.*

*They were a peaceful people, a people of faith. Their houses were small, the sky huge over the valley.*

*The land sustained them. They were happy.*

He'd hardly known where the Resistance would take him. Never had he envisioned a time, a place, a life such as this, turning, year by year, in the passing seasons of this valley, among this faithful people, these placid fellow-helping time passengers, for whom life was the work, the cooking, the breaking of bread, the tending of home fires, the sky-staring, the love-making, the sleeping that every day unfailingly brought them.

Still, the Resistance, having started out so far away, under such different circumstances, in the body of what seemed to be a wholly different man, a man with a different name — that Resistance lived on. It was still in him here, but now it consisted, strangely, of all of this. Somehow it always had.

It had led him, finally, to peace.

Had one road brought him here, Jikan sometimes wondered, or had he, somewhere he could not recall, stepped off the road, stopped believing in it, and in doing so come to understand, at last, the nature of true resistance?

That the road had never been.

That there is no road.

So often a valley is a place of passage. In this valley, though, there was no thoroughfare, no stream of passers-through, no way leading on to elsewhere.

There were footpaths, hoof trails, a branching of ways.

*Such a place is a terminus to some, a destination to others. For Jikan and his people, it was their living place. Not the only place, surely, but also more than only a place. No circle was drawn to cordon it. It was place in itself.*

*Things both moved and stood still in the valley. Things grew and were harvested. People laughed and coughed. Villagers aged and passed away. Babies grimaced and kicked.*

*Time did its work.*

*The large sky changed and changed.*

*The people neither waited nor planned.*

*From time to time there were hardships, but no particular cause to dread them. Any person could leave the valley and "move on," but none did. Why would you? For what?*

*The people's dialect contained no verb meaning "to arrive."*

*Once upon a time you would have died for a road. The road had never been.*

.   .   .

# 6.

# Works Lost :
## The Private Papers
## of G. P. Leed

"We must attribute part of our delight, part of our sense of the unfading life in this immortal book, to the ever-present traces of the human element which preserve it from a lifeless perfection. Some of these, in our age of mechanical printing, may seem faults; if we take any page at random we find a sprinkling of bent or broken sorts, dotless *i*'s, an *e* or *a* with a blotted bowl, letters over-inked or under-inked, raised, dropped, or slanted, a deliberate haphazard choice of level or sloping hyphens, a curved line or uneven line-ending, perhaps a short or long page due to miscalculation of copy or the need to introduce a woodcut. In this interplay of purpose and chance, care and carelessness, skill and fallibility, is the secret of the life in an artifact: we have been admitted to eternal moments in the autumn of 1499, when this book was produced by human hands and brains and man-made tools."
—*Hypnerotomachia Poliphili*, commentary
*Reference unknown.—Ed.*

\*

"I am my own best witness that the dolphin and anchor are my constant companions; for I have accomplished much by delay and continue to do so."
—Aldus Manutius, 14th October 1499

\*

*All evidence suggests that Leed intended to use the image above, borrowed from the 15th-century Manutius (an unknown personage), as the insignia for the Literary Resistance.*—Ed.

\*

It occurs to me that the artist's role is, essentially, only this: to communicate a distinct impression of <u>overabundance</u>. No matter how long a life you're given, no matter how storied your many creations, you must show how much, inexorably, you will leave undone. The true artist: not one who <u>accomplishes</u> but one who <u>begins</u>.

*Festina lente.* Make haste slowly.

The close of your life's work must be something more than a resignation or abandonment of your over-large task — it must be an invitation to continuance. Through all good work there runs a thread that is never severed. Between one artist and another, between lifetimes, the thread lies waiting.

*

*Un travail alimentaire*: work for buying food.
    I must do some, somehow.

*

Memory: very early — Kindergarten? — an earthquake in the schoolroom. Cupboard doors and drawers flew open. A teacher spilled backward in her chair. Children scrambled under tables.

*

Dream: On a river cruise, through lush and long-civilized countryside, a very appealing, peaceable region. The weather, however, was poor. I was idly complaining to another passenger when an elderly couple behind me overheard. A retired pair, pleasure-seekers. The old man stepped forward and standing very close to me said solemnly, in measured words boomed out like a bell, "We all must enjoy the time we are given!"

*

"There is beauty to be found in everything, you only have to search for it; a gasometer can make as beautiful a picture as a palace on the Grand Canal, Venice. It simply depends on the artist's vision." —Algernon Newton
*Reference unknown.—Ed.*

*

Whenever the sun returned, the frosted fenceposts and barn roofs would steam.

*229*

The narrowing down, the scraping away to the basis,
the constantly reducible nature of one's material, the
quest through fewer and fewer options, the steady
resolve to persist toward that last gratifying sense of
inevitability, the necessity of removing all alternatives
in the interest of purity and finality and natural
resolution, the need to know the thing has become the
only thing it could ever wish to be, has had its <u>allness</u>
fulfilled and every part of its destiny realized — all this,
and yet knowing all the time the vast and innumerable
alternate endings. This is what unites art-making and
the process of living a life. How alike they are. How
alive one is, consequently, when working well.

*

"Grace to be born, and to live as variously as possible."
—Frank O'Hara, his epitaph
*Frank O'Hara: unknown personage.—Ed.*

*

"Go thou my incense upward from this hearth."
*Quotation unknown.—Ed.*

*

The novelist needs a degree of mystical secrecy about
his subject. In the Networked world, with 'all
information' seemingly equally available, we say the
possibility of such secrecy is lost. The attention of the
novelistic imagination, it is believed, is inevitably
scattered by the broad equality of accessible data and
the loss of each given subject's secret allure.

But these suppositions are absurd — a massive

fallacy. The undigitized world of course <u>exists</u>, never to be exhaustively explored or conclusively framed by any combination of media. It is our vision that has shrunk, not the world.

*

The Network's bias: an omnipotent favoring of 'trends.' The tireless automated correlation of mere keywords. Creates, all but instantaneously, the latest phenomenon, 'happening,' 'news event,' etc. Effect: An illusory, narrow, paranoiac picture of the world, born of ciphers and terms, so-called 'data' which breed at speed, like rabbits.

*

It's a matter of the differences between philosophy and propaganda. The former consists of questions and conduces to enrichment, expansion, via uncertainty. The latter concerns itself entirely with 'answers,' pugnacious surety via incessant repetition, sometimes dogmatic but more often enticingly disguised (i.e., as personal empowerment).

We believe we choose the data, but the data choose us.

*

The accumulative force of brutal repetition — the means by which any base or lyrical platitude may seem to acquire significance and insight. The 'echo-chamber': constantly sublimating one banality after another until individual sensibility is altogether brutalized.

*

The public penchant for melodrama.

\*

"His desire for internal sovereignty, sharp sense of dignity, admiration of beauty, passionate facing of the world, search for tensions and bedazzlements — all this helped him attain independence in the face of the totalitarian pretension of modern thought." —Wojciech Karpinski, intro to Gombrowicz Diary

*Karpinski, Gombrowicz: Unknown personages.—Ed.*

\*

He was powerless, of late, to do much but revisit novels he'd read years before.

\*

This morning again — again! — Rosetta. She arrived early and stayed on much longer than ever before. We lay in bed while the sun climbed high across the window, clutching each other. She seemed, I thought, to not want to leave, and I cared little to get up and go to work. There was, in our indolence, a kind of drawn out musical resolution. Something valedictory about the visit. I buried my face long in her hair. Even before she'd gone I was nostalgic for the smell.

Rosetta, key to previously unattainable understanding. Rosetta, index to all the lost languages of life, everything that might have been. Oh my heart! That I've never known your name matters nothing to me.

\*

The things which, as we go on living, fall away from us. The large things, the loves, etc.

*

But also the little earthly things we keep and keep, never thinking we cannot keep them forever, until one day, quite without ceremony, we let them go, toss them out in the household trash with almost a feeling of relief, half-regretting we ever kept them. As if they were never artifacts. As if we can convince ourselves their loss makes no difference to us.

One such thing that comes to mind is that kitschy picture of Hamlet with his skull. It was a canvas reprint of some illustration striving for the style of Arthur Rackham. It hung in the entry of the lodging house in Lowell, its frame a gaudy plastic spray-painted gold. Tacky as it was, I loved that picture. The moment I first saw it, its meaning was clear. I looked and thought: It hangs there <u>for me</u>. I was remembering that story about Keats and his trip to the Isle of Wight — his finding so much significance in the Shakespeare portrait that hung in his hotel there. The landlady had given him the portrait to hang above his desk and in a letter home he wrote of his feeling that "a Good Genius" was presiding over him — "Is it too daring to fancy Shakespeare this presider?"

The Hamlet picture was for me — who else could it possibly be meant for? — and without a qualm I stole it off the wall. To me it seemed of such importance that when my landlady demanded I return it, I left in the middle of the night rather than doing so, even though it meant I'd given up my room.

This wasn't theft. I was the only reliable prophet of

my future, and I knew I had a right to that picture. It was mine.

I carried the picture with me for years. Even the thing's pictorial awkwardness (Hamlet in his ruffled collar had a mooning 12-year-old girl's face) could not deplete its significance.

We keep our little amulets. Talismans, totems, charms. They're useful, whatever one may believe. They're one more form of resourcefulness, which is the true challenge confronting us always. Always to be resourceful — in one's attentions, one's looking and listening, and in one's privations. Above how many desks did I hang that tacky frame? We must hold onto things. It preserves us somehow, this irrational need. For as long as necessary, it preserves us.

The picture is gone now. Finally some years ago I gave it up, I can't recall where. Sometimes, with an absurdly incommensurable sense of loss, I still miss it. *Arthur Rackham, Keats: references unknown. / Hamlet: a once-iconic protagonist from a novel now lost. / Shakespeare: a legendary playwright. Works lost.—Ed.*

\*

"A moment," we say, lifting a finger, pleading for patience, turning away or looking inward in thought. Un moment. Ein minuten. Often, too, we plead this way for a little silence. "A moment, a moment, please!" Always what is meant is something less than a minute, but often more than a minute is taken. The real plea is for a brief exception altogether from the laws of time.

\*

Disegnia Antonio, disegnia Antonio, designia e non perdere tempo!
*Quotation unknown (translation: Draw Antonio, draw Antonio, draw and don't waste time!).—Ed.*

\*

Reading in Berger about the contrast of human figures and animals in medieval painting. The humans are usually <u>restrained and anxious</u>, but the animals seem to <u>celebrate the present</u>. The animals' frolics are just that, while most human frolics are overhung with dread, with the sense of a guilt suppressed, a reckoning merely postponed. Berger says the humans are waiting, always 'waiting for the judgment which will decide their immortality.' Looking carefully, he says, you can see that the artists envied the animals.

The dangers of damnation of one kind or another have never gone away. You never learn to live without the dread. Any minute still, you can be condemned. And so that old condition of wanting feverishly to turn every moment to account. Of constant and grinding action in the effort to escape a great squandering.

\*

But oh, those minutes and hours of the divine slow burn in which a book, a story is made. With persistence, you get there. It does come, like a near beatitude. And only then does the dreading go. Then you are the dog, the horse, the lion of the medieval painting. No damnation endangers you.
*Berger: reference unknown.—Ed.*

\*

He said he loved the language of natural ruin. The
wrapping of words around the line breaks in a sonnet.
He understood the sadness of mountains, of rivers
buried in forests, the Cartesian loneliness of maps. It
overwhelmed him to consider the infinite secrecy of
existence in all forms and settings. The ancient privacy
of fish in a wilderness pool, or the long-winged fly in
the high whorl of a tree. The parallel kingdom of
stones, pinnacles sheathed in ice, realms of darkness
underwater. Even the lives of inanimate things. The
dusty cup forgotten in the dead man's attic. Anything
duration could touch.

*

"He could not see his way past the cost of the moment."
—Bruce Olds
*Reference unknown.—Ed.*

*

There were skeletons in the peaks, the jungles: of men,
of lions. The drowned creature's carcass bloomed algae
and fed nibbling sealife. The ribcage housed the
octopus. The shoulders of some birds were silver in
flight. The wind at night could snap like a dark sail in
its riggings. Under prairie grass and chaparral old
Indian paths still marked a way. In the marble flooring
of some cities were ruts sunk three inches deep, grooves
of weighted wagons from millennia past. Imperial
capitals and frontier towns submerged in burnt strata.

*

He said he'd long wanted to understand the innocence
that can carry a lie, the dark lines laid down to claim

ownership, identity, to create a principality and the readiness to die for it. He believed he could understand hate. The soldier came to hate at some level the comrade entrenched beside him. You hated because you wanted to love. Because the prospect of loss was a ruthless constant. Nations were no different, societies. What you hated were the unnatural constructs — the country you were dying and killing for. And you hated the natural constraints — isolating desert, seas, constriction of the mother tongue and the home religion. These made love impossible. The strangulated need to love grew into hate, until you believed you could love a nation, a theory, and kill for it.

*

Time, he said, was real. But a year never truly turned — *tomorrow, perhaps, I wish, I should, I was.* Age was a quality of air. Death a question of soil. Glass fogged over, birds swatted and scattered, blown leaves scuttered in street and grass, and the weathered nail — bent and red — screeched when pulled for salvaging from the wood.

*

What do you gain?
What do you give up?
What comes back from ancient days?
What tools have you made and how may they turn against you?

*

"The poet, the artist, the sleuth — whoever sharpens our perception tends to be an antisocial; rarely 'well-

adjusted,' he cannot go along with currents and trends. A strange bond often exists among antisocial types in their power to see environments as they really are."
—M. McLuhan

*

Again today the Bureau came calling. Their second visit in a matter of weeks. It was a different agent this time. No mention was made of Agent Keith. This is where their operations are so chillingly sensible. This way, you see, the process of harassment never becomes personal. The Bureau is keenly aware of my visits to Kasden, and probably our correspondence — and now too there is Norah to concern them. The man who came today, an Agent H., was all process, purely officious. The whole thing seemed to be, for him, a mere formality. The way he stood here in my room hardly looking around, asking one and then another question, having already anticipated my every reply — from this I came to understand how much they already know. Nothing new could come of our conversation, but protocol demanded the conversation be had. I am, to them, a matter whose resolution is well underway.

All questions regarding Kasden I evaded, exactly as they could expect. And as much as I was asked about him, there could be no doubt that the subject at hand was <u>me</u>.

*Leed was correct. Among the few members of the nascent Resistance, he had become the Bureau's main object of attention. The reason for this appears to have been mainly practical: between V. Kasden, Norah ----, and himself, he*

*alone could still be relieved of moderate privileges and*
*comforts, his living quarters in particular.  —Ed.*

✳

They've caused the Doctor a great deal of agitation. He
doesn't know what to make of me now, poor man. Will
I become far more trouble than I am worth? He's left it
to me, by his silence and signs, to say what we will do
about all this. I think of that silver bullion he showed
me, his helpless wish to go on securely, in solvency and
peace, through the collapse that lies ahead. When it
comes, what will even precious metals be worth? The
Doctor doesn't know, nobody knows, but he wants to
batten down, he's securing the riggings.

Haven't we looked at each other all the time, he and
I, with only the most tentative resolve? Passersby, the
Doctor and me.

✳

He was amazed sometimes that he'd survived so long.
Survival, as a feat accomplished by anyone, amazed him.

✳

"Q: Did you receive orders from anyone to paint
Germans, jesters, and the like in this picture?
A: No, sirs. But I received orders to adorn the picture as
I thought fit, and I saw that it was a large one and
could hold many figures.
Q: Is it not for you artists to add to your pictures such
figures as are fitting and in keeping with the subject
and with the principle personages? Or do you follow
your own pleasure and imagining, without restraint or
judgment?

*239*

A: I make my pictures with befitting consideration, as my mind can understand the matter.

Q: Does it appear fitting to you that at the Last Supper of Our Lord there should be introduced jesters, drunkards, Germans, dwarfs, and suchlike scurrility?"

—The inquisition of Veronese, transcript, 1573 *Reference unknown.—Ed.*

*

Etc., etc.

*

Yes, one falls in love with one's present work. And isn't this as it should be? Isn't it necessary? Why would we expect or demand anything else?

# 7.

# In Country

# JIKAN

*They pushed across our threshold waving their rifles and fired through the roof.*

*My daughters clung to me on the floor. Splinters and clay rained upon us.*

*They ordered my wife to cook and jabbed her with their guns. Afterward they sprawled in the house vulgarly, eating our food and spitting upon us and glaring at us with their empty black eyes. When they had eaten the food from our house they pulled my wife up from the floor beside me and led her outside.*

*The girls clung to me on the floor.*

*These devils slaughtered my wife in the dooryard. Neema got up and ran to her mother and they slaughtered the child too. It was then I told Fatima to flee. She was very afraid but I made her go. At the back of the house were the boards that she and her sister had loosened in their play. She slipped through and ran as I told her. To the hills, I told her. Don't stop. Her body was all fear, but she went without crying, I saw her disappear in the darkness.*

*They stand over me in the room where I now sleep alone. They wave their rifles today as always.*

*We will kill you all, they say. It is God's wish.*

*And at the front, one waves no rifle in my face but heavy sticks. You will use these like we tell you, he says.*

*Kill me, I say, kill me you are right it is God's wish.*

*In my fingers I turn the pink plastic beads, counting prayer by prayer. Kill me, is my prayer. But the one at the front rips the beads from my hand and tosses them away. Do not pray like one of us. You will use these like we tell you. Maybe it will kill you and we will all be happy.*

*His eyes are very black. In his face is the belief that he understands mercy.*

*Behind him the others laugh.*


*They bind my feet. They throw me like a dead one into their truck with the bodies. I recognize the face of my neighbor's wife. Her head is bare, her hair spills like the death over her nose and eyes, her open mouth drinks the dust that swirls from the wheels.*

*The truck roars across the rocky country to the village boundary, to the mountain where the great Gods stand. For a week these devils have lurked about shooting their rifles. My neighbors say these devils will destroy the great Gods. They keep shooting the Gods with their guns and throwing their grenades and firing their mortar rockets and finally yesterday they tried with the shoulder missiles. Still the Gods stand. These devils are like ants at the Gods' feet. The guns and the missiles are little sparks, no more.*

*The biggest God stands tall as the mountain. The smaller one is still half so tall. Together they watch over the valley. Since before our people can remember they have watched. When my wife's grandfather was a boy they stood just here*

*like now. He looked east and always saw them. They watched*
*when the other Armies came. And in the times when our*
*countrymen killed each other in the streets. And they watched,*
*the Gods, many times of trouble before all that.*

*They are forbidden, say the devils. God has no rivals and*
*only infidels would seek to build such idols. For this reason*
*too these devils have made all music forbidden. They think*
*they can make my people forbidden. They think God smiles*
*upon them and breathes bullets on everyone else. But it's these*
*guns that breathe bullets and God murders no one.*

*They pull me from the truck and unbind my feet and lead me*
*to the foot of the small God.*

*They carry boxes filled up heavy. They drop the boxes in*
*the dirt. We stand in the sun and dust. I can hear gunfire*
*from the village like thin hands clapping. These devils tread*
*the earth waving their rifles, smoking.*

*A second truck rumbles across the rocky country. Dust*
*follows it. The devils make noises between each other. In the*
*second truck six more men from the village lie bound at the*
*feet. I know each one. Each one's family was slaughtered. The*
*devil who carried the heavy box goes to the second truck,*
*shouting. Six villagers? Only six? What foolishness is this?*

*They untie the feet of the other villagers. These devils push*
*us into a line. From the trucks they pull long garment cloths*
*off the bodies of killed ones. They say, Tie these into sashes*
*about your shoulders. Then into the cloths they shove the*
*heavy sticks. T-N-T say the sticks.*

*The devils produce from the trucks long hand-drills for*
*each of us. The drills are blunt and narrow but it is clear we*

*are meant to bore holes in the sandstone. The devil in front waves in vulgar manner to the God in the mountain behind us. The other devils wave the same.*

*Climb, they say. Climb!*

*They are very small below. Their noises shrink to almost nothing. I see my country now, as the great God has seen it for centuries before my term on earth arrived. It is all one land.*

*I have drilled many holes. I have set the charges. We wake or sleep together, this God and me.*

*Now, in these moments, up at this height, I can hear it. The sound, very clear, of the God's breathing …*

. . .

# 8.

# Works Lost :
## The Private Papers
## of G. P. Leed

Our hands take hold of the air of speech, the page carries it forward. It's not only breath, an endless passing by. The tools are yours already.

*

"If a right to a secret is not maintained then we are in a totalitarian space."—Derrida
*Reference unknown.—Ed.*

*

We are collectors, keepers, archivists, researchers, referrers, recorders, and amanuenses. We are writing it down, always we are writing it down. We have not forgotten the value of transcription. Where would we be without the distillating pen? So much would flow over us always, a sea, larger than memory. To get it down, to sink one's bottle at the source, to carry some of it off for taste, those minerals, the slaking of thirst. You look at us and wonder, why do they always write? What can they do with them, those caught words? And of you we wonder, how can you let them go? Are you listening? Are you listening at all?

*

"One of the expedients which the curate and the barber bethought themselves of, in order to aid their friend's recovery, was to stop up the door of the room where his books lay, that he might not find it, nor miss them

251

when he rose; for they hoped the effect would cease
when they had taken away the cause; and they ordered
that if he inquired about it, they should tell him that a
certain enchanter had carried away study, books and
all."

*

Commit these things to the carriage of time, of
revisitation. Make it all material. Render it up and run
your fingers over, think through it again and say to
yourself, ah.

*

"Two days after, Don Quixote being got up, the first
thing he did was to go visit his darling books; and, as he
could not find the study in the place where he had left
it, he went up and down and looked for it in every
room. Sometimes he came to the place where the door
used to stand, and then stood feeling and groping about
a good while, then cast his eyes, and stared on every
side, without speaking a word."

*

Time quickens now, running out. Whoever you are, I'm
afraid we must part company. But the thing we've left,
and what lasts here where we meet — and maybe
beyond these edges — is the silence. Tongue of our
readerly mind, a living language after all. Strangers, in
this we stay intimates.

*

There is justice in paths and their crossings. How many

in every crowd have we seen before and forgotten? From now on let us look for one another.

*The private papers end here.—Ed.*

# 9.

# In Country

# STONE GOD

*Breathing...*
  *breathing...*
  *breathing...*

*The valley is quiet.*
  *The sun falls where, for a little while, there were houses*
*and fields.*
  *Nothing stirs.*

*In some trees, however, the bees are at work.*
  *Slowly, slowly, the power that once made apricots is*
*gathering.*

*In time, across the valley below, the sound of music comes*
*faintly.*
  *Singing.*
  *Soft strumming.*
  *And down there, very small, very slow, a man is traveling*
*afoot.*
  *He's making his way over the wrecked land.*
  *He carries an instrument.*

.   .   .

# ADDENDUM

*This letter was recovered secretly from Market Optimization Bureau files.*

Dear Kasden,

We knew it would go this way, it's no surprise to either of us. The main thing is, as ever, to keep at our work. Having drawn deeper and deeper into this terrain, we'll one day glance back to see its surface, from that distance, all smooth again. It is only the day that is difficult, but life is more than a day. More, even, than a mere series of days.

I'm writing something new, called <u>Partisans</u>. I'll send it when it's done.

—G